The Unfa

Tales of the City
1

The Unfading Flower

Tales of the City

Michael
Summerleigh

Dancing
Wolf
Press

Dancing
Wolf
Press

The Unfading Flower

THE UNFADING FLOWER
Tales of the City

When the City Sang in a Voice of Stone & Steel

The Sword of the Defender

The Artlessness of Loving

Of Silver Stars & a Siren Singing

Back Pages

Dreams of Nubian Splendour

Under a Mauve-Grey Moon

Tristesse

Fata Morgana

The Unfading Flower

Envoi: The Shape of Things to Come

When the City Sang in a Voice of Stone & Steel

for Beethoven and the Voodoo Child

Nicholas Wyndham double-locked the door of his house and, in turning to the narrow cobbled lane that ran through St John's Mews to the small circular court before his door, received the very distinct impression that something quite out of the ordinary would attend upon his outing that night. The weather was warm, but with a cool breeze at whiles springing up to dispel the sultriness of the day; the sky was a silver-shot mantle of black velvet overhead, where even the tallest spires of the City could do no more than raise themselves up, like yearning fingers striving to touch something infinitely more grand than themselves. Nicholas—who was known to admirers as Nicky, and to his friends as Windy—felt this was as it should be. Heaven and Earth were, to his mind, entirely disparate spheres where the works of Man stood apart from those of the gods, and for the former to have actual physical contact with the latter would have been nothing short of sacrilege.

However, as he stood in the courtyard, with his key-ring yet poised on its downward course to the pocket of his frock coat, a sense of quiet excitement seemed to intrude upon his normally placid temperament; in so doing, it disturbed somewhat the pleasant sense of anticipation with which he had left his house to seek the company of friends at a small nearby cafe, yet the disturbance itself was not at all unpleasant, just a little bit puzzling.

For a moment he stood unmoving in the starlight—the office towers that ringed the Mews effectively hid the face of the bright three-quarter moon from his sight—with his flaxen-haired head cocked to one side, listening to the hum of traffic out on the Boulevard, the faraway murmur of voices from open windows in neighbouring houses. These sounds were commonplace enough, as was the scent of the apple blossoms on the trees that stood on the perimeter of the courtyard, and the faint tang of motor oil and exhaust fumes that would occasionally intrude upon cloistral setting of the Mews.

But Wyndham felt something else, something strange and indefinable; though he recognised it not at all, could not begin to guess where it might come from, nevertheless it struck upon his artist's sensibilities and filled him with a dizzying rush of near-childlike wonderment.

And then, as quickly as it had come, the sensation was gone, leaving him to stand with a small frown of thwarted concentration across his forehead and a slightly bemused almost silly smile upon his lips.

He shrugged, put his hands into the pockets of his coat and went on his way, his boots scuffing faintly at the timeworn stones. Just off the courtyard, where it narrowed on its way to the Boulevard, a bearded man sat before his door regarding a blank rectangle of white canvas that stood on an easel before him.

"Evening, Nicholas," the bearded man said, tentatively applying his brush to a splash of colour on the palette held in his other hand. "Ever try painting by starlight?"

"Good evening t'you, Robertson," he replied, "and no, I can't say I have. Then too, I've never tried painting by any light. Is it important?"

Robertson turned his head and gazed up at him with a pair of piercing dark eyes darkened further by heavy brows effectively blocking any errant strands of illumination from above.

"I'm not sure yet," he growled, frowning. "I've never tried it before...but tonight...for some strange reason...I thought I'd have a go at it. The thing is, I'll be damned if I know where or how to begin. I got this feeling a little while ago, and though I've never had any kind of trouble conjuring up an image of something I've felt, this one's like nothing I've run into before..."

Wyndham nodded sympathetically. Robertson was the only person of his acquaintance who addressed him by an unmodified version of his given name. It lent the man a somewhat special distinction, and went a long way in softening the brusque tone that often crept into his dealings with others.

"Well...good luck with it then anyway," he said earnestly, continuing on down the lane. Over his shoulder he called back to him. "I'll be sure to raise a glass or two of wine on your behalf...anoint the pavement...just to add a bit of something to the effort."

He heard Robertson mutter *Damned pagan!* into his beard, and grinned to himself. A half dozen steps further and he saw a pair of ghostly green eyes winking at him from the darkness of an archway, that swiftly materialised into a large whisper-grey shadow that leapt up onto the stone wall beyond it. Wyndham approached the creature slowly, with the air of a courtier before his sovereign, and reached a long-fingered hand to scratch him gently between the ears. The green lamps went out, and a rumbling purr came from its throat as Wyndham moved his fingers down through the thick fur of his chest.

"And good evening to you, Sir Grim," he said softly. "How go things in the Kingdom of the Cats?"

Grim the Grey declined to make answer to the question, preferring to devote his full attention to the ministrations upon his royal person. Wyndham chuckled, ran his hand one last time across the feline's flank, and went on his way.

"Someday I'll learn the language you speak, your Highness," he whispered. "Who knows what secrets I'll learn then..."

At length he came to the end of the Mews, where the cobbles became granite-flecked pavement and the Church of St John the Defender raised up its modest battlements over the brief side street that led to the Boulevard. There he found the stout figure of Father Ambrosius in white-cassocked surveyance of the world, at the foot of broad double doors that rose up to twice his height, hinged and studded with ancient iron. Nicholas raised a hand in silent greeting, nodding politely as he passed by.

"God go with you, my son," said the priest solemnly.

"And all of them with you, Father," replied Nicholas.

"Bloody pagan!" exclaimed the cleric.

Nicholas turned and walked backwards as he answered the charge.

"A peaceful pagan, at worst, Father," he laughed. "Come by some afternoon and we'll see what can be done for the mutual salvation of our souls."

"Hell will freeze over, young man—!" began Father Ambrosius.

"Yes...I know...!" cried Nicholas. "And no doubt Lord Scaly-Tail will go on ice-skates. All the same, I think my wine cellar will tempt you in the end, Father..."

He didn't have to look for the smile he knew had lit upon the priest's face. Theirs was a slightly contentious ritual belonging solely to the pair of them. He waved a farewell and faced forward again, his legs moving him quickly over the pavement, his strides becoming longer with each step as though to challenge the pace of the motor cars that sped by him on the Boulevard. And then the feeling that had come to him outside his door, the sense of quiet excitement, came to him again, more strongly this time, and he stopped...ears straining for a sound... eyes gone bright and dreaming...turned inward to seek the nature and form of whatever it was come to visit upon him.

Again it lasted only long enough for him to recognise it before it fled away a second time, swiftly, like a water sprite surprised by the loutish stumbling of a mortal lost in some Faerie forest. Wyndham came back to the world around him dazedly, but with a firmer conviction that something odd and possibly miraculous was to befall him before the sun would rise again over the City.

A group of people—three couples dressed for an evening at the theatre perhaps—walked past him, and he smiled...foolishly...causing them to look at him uneasily before disdain fell about them like a cloak once they had taken in the dated elegance of his attire. They hastened away, and Nicholas began to wonder...

"Am I then the only one?" he asked himself aloud. "But no...there was Robertson...so it must be something..."

He pondered the question in a very serious manner all through the time it took him to walk the seven blocks to the cafe. On any other summer night, if he was early for a trysting with his friends, he would have stopped along the way—sat awhiles on the wooden benches encircling the fountain in Emperor's Park, or wandered lazily through the honeyed environs of the Emerald Gardens—but on this night his usual distractions did not tempt him to stray or linger. The question he had asked of himself became one of a burning urgency, and it was with a decidedly desperate air that he came to the terrace of the Silver Rose, where he sought out his comrades and breathed a sigh of relief when finally he was seated among them.

"Windy would you please do *something* to make poor Andrew smile?" pleaded Diana, leaning across the table to bestow him a kiss of welcome. "It's a delicious night and I've gotten a place with the dance company of my dreams, but poor Andy's been thrown over by his lover and I can't celebrate properly with him looking so miserable."

She stood up with her hands on her hips and put a pout on her elfin-featured face, while Tom, Gareth and Brandywine echoed her plea, but with greater discretion and much less strident tones.

"We've done the best we can with him," said Gareth, leaning forward in his chair, "but the man refuses all comfort and has gone so far as *not* to be impressed by a perfectly marvellous drawing that Brandy finished today."

Gareth proceeded to dust the spectacles he wore for effect with the tasselled end of a flimsy scarf he wore for the same reason rather than any true sense of sartorial enhancement...shook his head of flaming curls in Brandy's direction, who proffered the said drawing for Wyndham's inspection.

"It's a self-portrait," she explained, though thus far no one of them had had the least trouble in identifying the subject as Brandywine demurely but unmistakably bereft of any clothing. The portrait was done in a manner that left very little to one's imagination.

"I think it's a lovely drawing," drawled Thomas, with a sparkle in his eye.

"Well you would!" replied Brandy without too much rancour. "But Windy is our *ultimum judicium*."

"Our what?"

"He's the one gets to say if it's good or not," she said, and looked to Wyndham.

"I think Tom is dead on the mark if somewhat lacklustre in his appraisal, Branny sweet, but I also think under the circumstances Andrew is well within his rights not be impressed or comforted by your lovely portrait."

Nicholas turned to Andrew, who was sunk down in his chair with an expression of near-tearful wretchedness on his pale features.

"Is it true?" he asked softly, putting his hands gently on either side of the other's face. "Has that tasteless and thoroughly insensitive son of a screamer given you the gate?"

Andrew looked up and nodded.

"He told me to pack up and get out by noon tomorrow," he said miserably. "I know he's a class A bastard, Windy, but it doesn't change things much."

Nicholas nodded. "You're still mostly head over heels anyway," he said sympathetically. "It doesn't change anything like that at all...but you know you're much too good for him, Andy, and a little bit of time *will* change things. You'll see. Meanwhile, you can move in with me until whenever, and write your brains away on the topic of faithless love."

Andrew nodded again, seemed to brighten somewhat.

"Most of last night already," he said, with a trace of enthusiasm creeping into his voice. "I finished three poems and began a story."

"So this ex-lover is good for something after all," Nicholas grinned. "And thrown over or not I say you owe Diana some sort of congratulatory, a convincing show of appreciation for Brandy's finer attributes, and a reading of the aforementioned verse immediately, to be accompanied by copious amounts of wine procured at my own expense."

A chorus of approval greeted the pronouncement and, as the Silver Rose had become quite busy during the course of their discourse, Diana took it upon herself to go in search of someone to attend to their needs. An hour later, Nicholas sat back from the lively—and increasingly inebriated—conversation of his friends and, for the third time that evening, became aware of the *strangeness* that was threading its way through the normal sights and sounds and smells of the City. Again he felt the quiet excitement rise up in him, this time immeasurably stronger, and light-headed with a full litre of wine to his own credit he found the flood of sensation approaching *delicious*...which in turn puzzled him further...

"But why am I the only one...?" he murmured aloud.

The moon hung in the sky like a huge silver platter—he saw now it was full rather than merely three-quarters so—smiling down upon the City, illuminating the small chaos of motor cars on the Boulevard, the faces and clothing of those who strolled casually, stopping briefly at shop windows, or finding refreshment at the myriad cafes along its length.

He heard it in those moments, something that seemed to come from afar but drew nearer and nearer—through the voices of the café's patrons...the roar of automobile engines...the clangour of horns...through it all amid these sound was a deep and subtle thrumming, no louder than any of the other sounds but now unmistakeable...insistent.

"If I were to endlessly bow the bass string of my cello it might sound something like it," he said in amazement. "But where is it coming from? What's causing it?"

He became aware that his friends' conversation had ceased, that they all were staring at him with broad smiles on their faces.

"A miracle has come to pass," announced Tom with a flourish of his wine glass. "Windy is three sheets to the wind and discussing it with himself."

Nicholas looked at each of them in turn, seeking some indication that they had noticed the sound...*something*...

"Can't you hear it?" he demanded of them

"Hear what, Windy?" asked Diana with concern. "Have you really gone stinko on us?"

"No...no...listen!" he cried. "Everything is the same, but there's something different going on...underneath all of it..."

He repeated his thought regarding the bass string of his cello and watched their faces become masks of concentration as they tried to pierce through the commonplace sounds of the City and find whatever it was he was talking about.

"You *are* drunk," said Diana sadly, shaking her head and refilling his glass. "Do have more wine, dear. I'm sure whatever it is will go away soon."

"Gareth? Tom? Andrew...?" he cried. "Don't any of you hear it?"

"I think maybe I *do* hear something..." said Brandywine suddenly. "It's a humming noise...like a giant bumblebee."

Diana snorted sceptically.

"You've just decided you want to sleep with Windy tonight because he said such nice things about your *portrait*," she said a tad derisively. "You needn't be such a gush about it..."

Brandywine blushed furiously.

"That's not why I said it!" she said indignantly. "I did hear something."

"We'll all be horribly jealous if you do Branny," observed Tom soberly. "And Diana will be jealouser still..."

THE UNFADNG FLOWER

Diana glared daggers at him, but said nothing because Nicholas had silently gotten to his feet and gone to stand on the street side of the railing that enclosed the terrace. Without a backward glance he began walking up the Boulevard and disappeared around a corner.

"Where on earth is he off to?" puzzled Gareth, as Diana's outstretched hand alerted him to the desertion.

"Well I think we should go after him," said Brandy.

"Of course," smiled Tom.

"I think we should follow him too," said Andrew, standing out of his chair and moving towards the gap in the railing. 'Even if Windy's not drunk he's acting awfully strange tonight."

It became the general consensus of those who chanced upon them that evening that there were six extremely bizarre creatures abroad in the City that night—a ragtag raucous procession of young people...five following one...who were old enough to know better than to wander about in shameless intoxication, prancing along in patched trousers, threadbare coats, dancer's tights and flimsy ragged skirts.

Nicholas led the procession in a fever of excitement, alternately running and plodding, stopping at whiles to cock his head and listen to sounds no one else seemed able to hear, his hair gone wild and windblown, his eyes dazed and unseeing. At one point he heard Gareth remark that he was probably just a little bit worn out from working so hard on a sonata composition, but Nicholas hadn't told any of them the sonata had been completed a week earlier. Occasionally—most often it was Brandywine—one of them would catch him up

11

during one of his plodding moments and ask him questions while gazing concernedly into his dreaming eyes, but he would shake his head once or twice and be off again in another direction.

He led them a merry chase through the night, circling the entirety of the Amaranth Palace; through the ancient archways that reared themselves up beside the Grand Canal; among the crumbling ruins of the Imperial Armoury; down to the river bank and thence around the harbour before turning back again into the concrete and glass canyons of the New City, where the office towers and government buildings glimmered in the silver splendour of moon and starlight.

When the rest of them were easy in their minds that Windy was neither a danger to himself nor others, their wandering became an impromptu celebration of sorts, the air resounding to laughter and snatches of song, street vendours responding to hurried calls for one treat or another, accepting airborne payment as the celebrants rushed off in pursuit of their mad prophet. And through it all, Nicholas heard the deep thrumming sound in his head, sought in vain for its source even as it grew into a rumbling thunder in his ears.

At length he brought them back to St John's Mews, past the now unwarded facade of the Church of the Defender, down the laneway and into the cobbled courtyard, where it was Thomas who halted their headlong career, and Diana who let them into the ground floor of the coach house by ferreting Windy's keys from the pocket of his coat. One by one they fell into armchairs, sprawled over divans, collapsed on the thick Travantine carpets on the floor, until only Nicholas stood on his feet, still listening intently, and Brandy—who did very much want to sleep with him that night—ignored the drowsy raillery of their companions as she took him upstairs to bed.

"You do hear it, Brandy, don't you?" he asked, as she undressed him in the glow of starlight creeping into the bedroom windows.

"I thought I did, Windy...before..." she replied softly, when he lay pale and helplessly dreaming on his bed, and she began to undress herself. "Now I'm not so sure...there were so many sounds, y'know, and everyone was laughing and talking..."

"But they were sounds that *we* made," he protested weakly. "I can scarcely believe it myself, but this one was so different..."

If his eyes had not been turned inward to see what he was hearing, he might have noticed Brandy standing over him, more lovely still than her self-portrait, wide-eyed with concern for him. Yet Nicholas remained blind to all but what seemed to thrum in his ears, even if he did sigh when she lay down beside him, joined the warmth and softness of her body to his slender frame. She curled herself into the shelter of his arms and went peacefully to sleep, listening to the beating of his heart, that sounded, all of a sudden, much like the humming of a giant bumblebee. And Nicholas stared upward, through the ceiling and skylights above, to the scatter of stars pricking the black vault of the night sky.

"I didn't know it was possible..." he whispered.

"...I can't imagine what's gotten into him tonight," observed Tom blandly from the depths of his armchair. "Windy's always been so level-headed about everything."

"Except maybe his music," yawned Gareth from the floor. "But that's to be expected, I suppose. We all get crazed over what we're doing on our own."

"Well we've got t'do *something* for him," said Andrew with a note of desperation in his voice. "He's always seen *us* through our bad times..."

"I imagine our Brandy is looking after him quite well enough," huffed Diana. She flung a long smooth-muscled leg over the back of the divan and sulked into a glass of claret she'd poured from the decanter on Nicholas' sideboard.

"Please do leave off being green, Di," drawled Tom. "It hardly becomes you, and I for one don't begrudge it either of them. Besides, I don't think Bran or Windy is up to much mischief tonight anyway. He's off with the fairies and she was half-asleep before we got here..."

Diana unflung her leg and sat up. "I just think it's a bit unfair," she said primly.

And Andrew said, "Brandy would be just as happy if it were you upstairs instead of her."

Gareth looked up with devilment in his eyes.

"There *is* one way to even things out a bit," he said puckishly. "And it's not like it would be the first time..."

The others looked at him and smiled in unison.

Nicholas roused himself up from a dreaming that had nothing to do with sleep, thinking the unthinkable, overwhelmed by the sound and excitement that had grown steadily with each passing minute.

"But why should it *not* happen?" he asked himself. "It's so old. Centuries of existence. If Time has been the agent of our own transformation, why should it not play the same role for all that we have done...or created...?"

He became aware of the fact he was not alone. Sweet Brandy slept in his arms, and he recognised the scent of Andrew close beside them, with Gareth and Tom and Diana at no great distance. He sensed rather than saw that he lay in the centre of a great tangle of arms and legs and naked bodies all of which belonged to his friends; that they had come to watch over him, to be close by whether he slept or not, and had fallen asleep themselves. He could taste the smell of them, smell the sweet acrid taste of their lovemaking, felt their warmth and heard the slow rise and fall of their breathing, the workings of their hearts...all joined together now in the measured thrumming that no longer could be denied...all in tune...

"There's one way I could be certain," he whispered.

Carefully, so very slowly so as not to wake any of them, he untangled himself from the tangle of his friends and went in search of his trousers and his cello. He went quietly downstairs, setting the instrument beside the front door while he transferred a captain's chair from the long oaken table in his dining room to the exact centre of the cobbled courtyard outside his door. Then he sat and listened...one last time...to be as certain as he could be of something he might once have thought to be impossible.

The last deepening darkness before the dawn seemed taut and electric with anticipation, crowding into the Mews in a kaleidoscope of jumbled perceptions. Somehow the moon had won itself free from the oncoming light of the sunrise, bathing the courtyard in one last brilliant wash of silver light; a murmur of motor car came from the Boulevard; the almost sultry heat was infused with a fresh coolness, a crispness of moist air that told him dewfall could not be far off. And through it came the insistent humming sound that had first come to him so many hours ago...

He bent over the neck of his cello, placed a finger cautiously on its bass string...drew his bow slowly across it and felt the cobblestones at his bare feet trembling with the sound.

"Yes..." he breathed, confident now, and having found the note, he closed his eyes and sought the chord, bowing it strongly...

"Yes!" he exulted again, feeling the cobblestones leap beneath him, resonating with joyous strength to match the resonant thrum of his cello.

"YES!" he cried a third time, and the chord became a flow of sound and the flowing of sound became a song that filled the Mews, thrilling the stillness away into an answering chorus as he played...blind with abandon and his head thrown back to drink the sound... feed it back into the oncoming day with his fingers.

And somewhere in the course of the night Hell must have frozen over, and the Devil gone downtown on ice skates, because the priest had come to stand in the courtyard with his face suffused in a light of almost divinely-inspired Joy...and beside him on the doorstep of his home a dishevelled Robertson stood with his empty canvas and frantically made brush strokes that seemed to mirror the sound rising up around them...and in the branches of the apple trees dozens of pairs of apple-green eyes winked down at them, and joined a rumbling chorale of cat-purrs to the song.

"Windy! What on earth—?" demanded Diana from the upstairs window, and he laughed when he saw the shocked expression on her face.

"You hear it now, Diana!" he cried, hurling his bow down upon the strings. "Now you hear it!"

And then she was gone from the window, and moments later they all poured from the door of his house in various stages of dress and undress—Brandy making do with a bedsheet—to crowd round him as he played on and on, laughing all the while.

"Can you believe it?" he shouted above the thrumming now roused up to its full and joyous power. "After all the years...echoing to all the sounds *we* have made...now...it recognises itself!"

And they looked on in amazement...listened...as for the first time in all the time it had stood yearning for the stars, the City sang in its own voice of stone and steel.

The Sword of the Defender

for Douglas Grass (1952-1992...done to Death by Hate

The door of the house in St John's Mews stood open to the dog-day heat of late summer as Andrew struggled with the intricacies of a spondaic heptameter. He sat on the divan in the front parlour surrounded by no less than seventeen crumpled balls of foolscap that evidenced his past failures to master it, and, framed by the somewhat perspiration-soaked strands of his jet-black hair, his pale features were creased by a frown of intense concentration.

To himself he wryly observed that the life of a poet, successful or otherwise, was no easy one, especially when the metrical feet belonging to an half-formed creation simply refused to follow their intended path; however, this unhappy bit of musing was interrupted—fortuitously, thought Andrew, with a guilty sigh of relief—as he heaved himself up from the couch to answer a persistent rapping upon the panels of the open door.

In the doorway, blinking away the blindness of bright August sun that shone down upon the cobbled courtyard of the Mews, stood a stout white-cassocked gentleman whose hairless dome of a head—fringed by a halo of fluffy white hair—and round, rather florid face, gleamed with a sheen of perspiration. A pair of kindly brown eyes peered at him from under shaggy white brows.

"Good afternoon," said Andrew, bowing slightly to acknowledge the visitor's obvious station as a man of the cloth, but unwilling, as a free-thinking poet of higher metaphysics, to accord him more honour than was his due. "Can I help you?" he inquired politely.

"Is this not the house of Nicholas Wyndham, the musician?" inquired the cleric hesitantly. He rocked back on his heels and looked first to his left and then to his right, as if Andrew's appearance had convinced him he had knocked upon the wrong door; that the one he sought must therefore live in a close proximity. Andrew smiled to reassure him.

"The very same," he said softly, "though Windy's not in just now. I think he's gone off to replace some strings on his bass viol, but he should be back within the hour. You're welcome to wait for him, if you like..."

The cleric's puzzlement vanished at once, and his sandaled feet scraped upon the doorstep as he hastened to accept Andrew's invitation to come in out of the sun.

"Thank you, I think I will at that," he said, moving into the relative coolth of the hallway.

"I'm Father Ambrosius, rector of the Church of St John the defender, just at the entrance to the Mews..."

He waved a pudgy hand in the general direction of his church, which stood just outside the archway leading into the Mews where it opened onto a side street off the Boulevard.

"Andrew MacKinnon, at your service," said the poet with another small bow. "Please come in and make yourself at home.

Would you like a glass of wine, or maybe some chilled fruit juice?"

Father Ambrosius allowed himself to be escorted into the front parlour where, with an intuitive sense that had yet to fail him, he sat himself in the most comfortable armchair of the three inhabiting the room. For a moment he was distracted by the paper wasteland made out of Andrew's poetic endeavours; then he turned his full attention back to him.

"A glass of wine would be splendid, my son," he said with an anticipatory smile. "Master

Nicholas has boasted to me once or twice of the quality of his cellar. I see no reason why I should pass up the opportunity to put his wine to the test."

"I think you will not be disappointed," said Andrew amiably. "This is a wonderful claret," he went on, pouring a glass from a decanter on the sideboard. "Windy's quite good with wine, as he is with just about everything. He says this is a '43, which means nothing to me, but it certainly does taste good."

"A '43...!" exclaimed the priest in appreciative tones. He took the glass from Andrew, held it up to the light, swished it about and then set the rim to his nose before taking a small sip. Seconds went by as he allowed it to caress his palate before swallowing.

"Marvellous," he sighed, "but an expensive vintage. Is your friend well-off then?"

Andrew shrugged. "One certainly would think so," he said noncommittally, "though I seem to remember Windy mentioning his family was quite old, with a rather large estate in the Carillon region..."

"And you, Master MacKinnon, if I may ask...?"

"Oh...well...I'm but a poor poet, at least in monetary terms," he smiled, nodding about at the litter of foolscap on the floor. "But really I guess I'm pretty wealthy...rich...because I have so many good friends."

They sat awhiles in silence, Father Ambrosius sipping his wine and Andrew observing him in turn, the parlour very still save for the hum of insects in the apple trees of the courtyard, and the occasional blare of a motor car's horn out on the Boulevard.

"Did you want to see Windy over anything of importance?" Andrew inquired at length. "Perhaps I can be of some help...while we wait for him...?"

The priest looked up from his glass.

"Indeed, now you mention it," he said warmly. "You see, I'm engaged in an investigation of sorts—for a short piece I intend to write for one of the church journals—regarding the very strange occurrence of three weeks ago...that night of mass hysteria, I imagine...half the City out wandering in the streets as if in search of some divine revelation."

"You mean when Windy made the City sing," corrected Andrew softly.

"Oh...?" said Father Ambrosius, raising both eyebrows with a quizzical air. "I was not aware Nicholas was actually responsible for it..."

Now Andrew smiled proudly. "We like to think so," he said, "meaning myself, Tom, Gareth, Diana and Brandywine. We were all here when it happened... snoozing away upstairs..."

"Really," said Father Ambrosius, his eyes lighting with excitement. He set his glass on a small tabouret of carved mahogany and, from somewhere within the voluminous folds of his cassock, extracted a small notebook and a pencil. "Perhaps I could impose upon you for your account of that night, and the impressions you received...?"

"Of course," replied Andrew, always more than willing to extol the virtues of his friend. "It all began when Windy joined us on the terrace of the Silver Rose..."

From there he went on to relate how all of them had noticed Windy's air of distraction, but generally chaffed him over his contention that there had been an odd, thoroughly unfamiliar sound underlying the usual sounds of the City; and how they had followed him all over everywhere as he searched for source of the sound.

"...And finally we ended up back here and Branny took Windy up to bed, and when Diana began to get jealous, I think it was Gareth who suggested we all go up and join them. And then we woke up a short time later...and then...well...Windy was outside in the courtyard with his cello and...you were there, weren't you...Father Ambrosius...?"

Somewhere during the course of Andrew's conclusion to the story, the priest had left off his frantic scribbling and begun to stare at the poet with something akin to absolute horror registering on his florid countenance.

"Master MacKinnon," he said slowly, "have I heard you correctly? Did you say first that this Brandy went upstairs with Nicholas...to his bed...and then the rest of your group *joined* them soon after...?!?"

Andrew nodded and a smile lit upon his lips as recollection of the night became bright again in his mind's eye.

"All of you...together...?" the priest asked again.

"Why...yes...of course," replied Andrew, now with an inkling of dismay in his voice. "It's a rather large bed and we were all quite comfortable...and then when we realised Windy was gone... why...Branny never even bothered to put her clothes on she just grabbed the bedclothes and..."

He stopped, now very much aware that the priest no longer was the excited and so very interested guest of a few moments before; that he had, in some way, grievously offended the priest, whose kindly eyes now glared at him coldly from a face flushed with some violent emotion.

"My son, do you know what you are saying?" he demanded. "Tell me, you all were clothed, of course...?"

"No, sir, I just told you. Brandy was so worried she never bothered to get dressed. It was a very warm night, after all..."

"All of you naked, in the same bed."

"Father, please," said Andrew, casting about in his mind for something that might calm the priest. "We're all good friends...family almost...and we'd done it many times before, when it was late and we were too tired to go home..."

"Many times!" cried Ambrosius. "All of you...together... naked...many times...?!?"

"Well...not *so* many times, truly," amended Andrew desperately. "I mean...Tom and Gareth are always trying to cosy up to Branny and Diana, I suppose...but they've stayed with Windy more times...and I have too...like now...because the man I was living with booted me out with no notice at all and Windy said it would be all right if I stayed here for a while...until I could find another place to live."

"You have slept in the same bed together?" said the priest hoarsely. "Just the two of you?"

23

"I was going to stay in the guestroom," said Andrew, "but he said it was no good me being lonely while I was here and...Windy's much kinder than most of the people I know...and sometimes he sings to me so I can go to sleep..."

Father Ambrosius leapt to his feet, his fists clenched and his eyes darting fire.

"I cannot believe I'm hearing this!" he cried. "That you admit it to me freely, with no shame whatsoever. Will you next say that you have known each other, engaged in sexual acts together?"

Father, Windy and I *do* love each other very much..."

Ambrosius' outraged stare became glazed and empty. "My God," he murmured passionately. "I pray thee I am not too late to save these two from their sins."

Andrew looked up at him in stunned surprise, his mouth hanging open stupidly, as if he simply didn't understand what he was hearing.

"What sins are you talking about, Father?" he asked in a trembling voice.

The cleric ceased his fervent supplication and a look of compassion suddenly overspread his countenance as he regarded the almost tearful young man before him.

"My son, is it truly possible you are unaware of your transgressions?" he asked softly. "That you do not know the word of the Church, indeed, the very Word of God with respect to what you have just told me?"

Andrew shook his head in helpless confusion.

"Father Ambrosius, I don't understand anything of what you're saying," he said honestly. "I thought you wanted to know what happened on the night Windy made the City sing, but all of a sudden you got so angry…"

"Andrew, have you not read the Scriptures? Did your parents not teach you…?"

"My father sent me away," he replied. "He told them I was a thief and a liar…and the book was full of horrors, people every bit as cruel as my father…"

"My son," said Ambrosius quickly, "you and Nicholas must come to me in my church and I will teach you to pray. And I will add my prayers to your own, that we may together win forgiveness for your immortal souls. The Lord is merciful to those of his flock who, out of ignorance, have strayed from the fold."

Again, Andrew shook his head. "I'm afraid I still don't understand, Father," he said quietly. "I know you mean well but…please tell me…what have Windy and I done wrong?"

The priest drew a deep breath and then sighed, as if to convey that while his patience and good will were of great depth and magnitude, they were not boundless.

"My son, it is written in the Scriptures that no man may lie with a woman out of wedlock without imperilling the immortal souls of both; but if a man should lie with another man, then in the eyes of God, they are surely damned for all Eternity."

Andrew raised up his dark brown eyes to the priest.

"But that's so stupid," he said.

Ambrosius blinked.

"I beg your pardon."

"I said that was stupid, sir, if you'll excuse me saying so," Andrew repeated himself.

"How can anyone's soul be damned or even imperilled by caring about someone else enough to hold him or make him feel loved? I may not be a religious person, sir, but I've always thought God wanted us to love each other."

The priest smiled wanly.

"Yes, my son, you are absolutely right," he said patiently, "but you must not take His words so literally. Two men...together...please do not be offended...but that is an abomination in His eyes, an insult to His love..."

"I think you're wrong, Father," Andrew said. "I think you're very wrong to say that. I love Windy and I know he cares about me—just like we care about and love Tom and Gareth and Diana and Brandy—-and we let each other know that by holding each other, and touching and kissing..."

"My son, you do not know any better and can be forgiven such words, but do not, I pray you, try to teach me, who am a servant of God and one of his many voices on earth, the meaning of His word."

"Well I'm sorry, Father," Andrew went on doggedly, "but don't tell me Windy's kindness is sinful because it's not. He always knows best about almost everything—you can ask any of our friends—and I should have died from hurt and loneliness if he hadn't let me stay here with him. And besides, who gets to decide what God's words mean...and how do you know God said anything at all about anything except for what you're telling me?"

"Andrew, I'm afraid your opinion of Nicholas Wyndham is somewhat biased," said Ambrosius sadly. Almost to himself he said, "I had no idea how far along the road to Perdition he had gone...but in truth, I have thought him very lost indeed, though I have held to my faith in God that someday he would come to his senses and turn upon the true path to his Lord."

"Windy lost!" cried Andrew incredulously. "Father, Windy's probably the only one of us who *isn't* lost. If I were to tell you how many times—"

"Silence!" thundered the priest. "For all your friend's great kindness he is a heathen...a pagan...a shameless sinner who flaunts himself before God and, I see now, goes even so far as to corrupt the souls of those around him!"

"That's the most ridiculous thing I've ever heard! Windy's never done a terrible thing in his life, and if you're too blind t'see that, and won't stop speaking of him in the way you just did—in his own house!—then I think you'd better go...now..."

"My son—"

"I'm not your son!" cried Andrew indignantly, "and I'm quite certain you know nothing about anything of importance!"

Ambrosius drew himself up to as great a height as he could manage and frowned terribly.

"You defy the Word of God?" he cried. "You will not repent of your sins...even seek to know them, and pray on your knees for the forgiveness offered to you, for the salvation of your soul?"

"I haven't done anything wrong and I don't need to pray for anyone's forgiveness!"

"You think so, eh?" said the priest tonelessly. "In that case I challenge you, Master Andrew MacKinnon. I challenge you to come to the Church of St John, and upon his sainted bones declare yourself before God, and there await a judgment that surely will come...if you have the courage...

"And as I do not think you possess that courage, I bid you good day...and farewell...and may the Lord have mercy upon your soul."

Ambrosius made the sign of the Cross upon his breast, and went stiffly from the house without another word.

Andrew was seated on the divan, staring blindly at nothing at all, when Nicholas' footsteps sounded on the cobblestones of the courtyard and he came through the door of his house.

"Andy I'm home!" he called out, flinging a canvas shoulder-bag onto the dining room table and stripping off his sweat-soaked coat. "Sorry to be so long but I ran into Brandy on the way back and...well...you know how she gets when she's excited about one of her paintings, so we went back to her place and got pleasantly pissed while I oohed and aahed over the canvas. It's really quite good she's getting better by the day and I'm starving what's for supper? Andrew...?"

He ran a puzzled hand through his pale blond hair and, in turning, found the poet almost exactly where he had left him. At once, his grey eyes grew dark with concern.

"Andy are you okay?" he said, walking over to sit beside him. I didn't think it was possible, but you look a lot less colourful than your usual I've-just-see-a-ghost-excuse-me-for-impersonating-a-sheet. I'm sorry I took so long...Andrew...would you please say something, just so I know you're not dead..."

Andrew turned his head slowly. As his eyes finally focused on Nicholas, he said, "Oh..." faintly. "Hello, Windy..."

"Thank the gods!" breathed Nicholas in relieved tones. "He yet lives and breathes and speaks to me in the manner of mortal men. Andy you scared me blue. Are you feeling sick?"

"No I'm fine, Windy...I think," he replied, picking up a handful of crumpled heptameters at his feet. "Father Ambrosius, from the church on the corner, called for you while you were out."

"Oh? What'd he want?"

"He said he was researching for an article he wanted to write about the City...when you made it sing..."

"Gods, Andrew! I hope you didn't tell him *that*. His opinion of me is shaky enough as it is."

"Yes...I know..." Andrew murmured, collecting up the rest of the foolscap crumples and taking them down into the kitchen. "He stayed for a while. I gave him a glass of wine. He got tired of waiting."

Nicholas followed him anxiously into the kitchen.

"Did anything else happen while I was gone? You're not looking very well at all, Andy. Why don't you lie down and I'll make supper..."

Andrew shook his head and addressed the dustbin.

"Nothing else...but I'm not very hungry, Windy."

"The devil, Andy! You've got t'eat supper. You're so damned thin now I keep expecting you t'turn sideways and disappear on me. How would I explain that to everyone, if they showed up here tomorrow and you'd faded away during the night?"

The poet looked at him with a strange, almost pained look in his dark eyes.

"I'm sorry, Windy," he whispered. "I guess I *am* feeling out of sorts. Could I...would you...just for a little while..?"

Wyndham's puzzlement increased a hundredfold, but he put his arms around Andrew at once.

For the most part they ate in silence, in spite of the fact that Nicholas had spent an hour in preparing Andrew's favourite slivered beef and mushrooms in a Beaujolais wine sauce, and a night had not gone by in the three weeks of his residence that Andrew had failed to be effusive in his thanks and praise of his friend's culinary efforts. However, as the night wore on and darkness fell over the City, the poet withdrew more and more into himself, until the musician's further attempts to find out what was bothering him received no answer at all.

"Whatever it is, Andy, I do wish you'd tell me," he said softly, "but if you'd rather not just now, that's all right too, I'll understand. Either way, it's time we went to bed..."

Andrew nodded miserably and dragged himself to his feet, but for the first time in the three weeks since he had moved in with Nicholas, slept alone in the guest room.

The next morning was grey and overcast, with dark stormclouds lowering over the towers of the City, the air thick and fraught with sharp crackles of electricity. When Nicholas came down to brew a fresh pot of breakfast coffee, he found

Andrew sitting at the kitchen table, once again staring blindly at nothing, though he seemed to be studying the rock garden that filled half their small enclosed back yard. His handsome features were drawn and heavy with fatigue, as if he had spent a thoroughly sleepless night.

"G'morning, Andy," he said softly. "Actually it stinks, but on days like this I suppose one ought to try to be optimistic."

He made the coffee, toasted half a dozen slices of bread, and brought the whole thing to the table along with spoons, cream and sugar, butter and a glazed pot of orange-and-lemon marmalade. Then he just stared at his friend while everything got cold.

"I missed you last night," he said.

"I missed you too, but I would've kept you awake all night."

"I wouldn't've minded that too much," replied Nicholas. "Then I could have slept through most of this wretched day."

A low rumbling sounded off to the west, followed by a slash of rain as the wind began to rise. When a fork of lightning stabbed across the sky seemingly sitting on their heads, both tensed in their chairs, waiting for the clap of thunder that came almost immediately, rattling all the window panes in the house. A large grey cat darted across the garden on immense furred feet, disappearing into a cave-like structure in the centre of the rockery. Moments later three more cats—a dainty calico, a short-haired tabby in russet and cream, and a rain-sodden black—followed the grey into the shelter.

"I don't imagine there'll be much in the way of court business for Grim today," observed Nicholas, referring to the first of the felines to seek shelter in his garden. "Not much of anything will be going on once the storm rolls in…"

Andrew nodded, picked up a slice of dry toast and began to nibble his way round the crust. Nicholas poured himself a mug of lukewarm coffee.

"Windy...is it wrong for me t'be the way I am?" said Andrew suddenly.

Windy took a swallow of the coffee and set the mug on the table. "What way is that, Andy?" he asked quietly.

The young man looked at him with red-rimmed eyes for an instant, then turned away quickly.

"I like girls a lot," he said "Di and Brandy...but not so I want t'be so close t'them...and do stuff...you know...?"

Nicholas nodded.

"And then there's people like you, who don't seem to mind whoever as long as whoever is somebody they like. And then there's me, Windy. Is there something wrong with me?"

Nicholas considered the question for a long time before answering, trying to determine what had caused his friend to ask about it in the first place.

"I've never really given it much thought, Andrew," he said. "You've always been... well...you've just been you, someone kind and gentle and a very dear friend. I don't think I could love you more than I do already, but I certainly couldn't love you less...especially over something like that. I wouldn't be much of a friend to you if I did."

"But is it wrong?" Andrew cried. "Is there something wrong with me?" and this time there was panic in his voice and he looked Nicholas straight in the eyes, pleading for an answer.

"Wrong for who, Andy? If we're talking about you, I'd say it was wrong only if it was making you unhappy...as it seems to be doing all of a sudden. But if we're talking about you in relation t'the rest of the world, I'd have t'say it's none of their bloody business. You can do whatever you damn well please, Andrew, and so long as you're happy and nobody else is getting hurt while you're about it, then it's okay. Right or wrong doesn't apply."

Andrew took a few minutes to digest that, and the small bites of his toast now the crust was gone. He stared out the window again, as the rain hissed and splattered on the glass.

"What about God, Windy?" he asked. "D'you think God thinks I'm doing something wrong?"

"I'm sure I don't have a clue what God thinks," Nicholas replied, "or if *He* even exists... or is a *He* t'begin with...but if he does think, Andy, and there's something in his head that's telling him there's anything wrong with you, then he's an idiot, and the opinions and values of idiots are worth less than...well...whatever *you* can think of that's totally worthless.

"Listen to me, Andy," he said slowly, as a strong suspicion dawned inside *his* head, "what went on between you and Ambrosius yesterday? If that old goat's been filling you up with claptrap about sins and this and that and the other damnation—"

"No, Windy, it's nothing like that," said Andrew hurriedly, which served only to confirm Nicholas' suspicions. "I don't know what started me off thinking this way. Maybe it was the poem I was working on...trying to put down in words some of the things I've been feeling about you...and the others..."

Nicholas shook his head ruefully. "Andy, I'm sure Ambrosius means well, but there are some things he doesn't begin to understand and likely never will, simply because he's the honest and dedicated priest that he is. To *understand* differently would be too much of a contradiction for him, more than he could bear as a challenge to his faith."

"Windy that's mostly what I tried t'tell him—!"

"I know," said Nicholas, "and it made about as much sense to him as one of Robertson's paintings. Just let it go, Andy. It's not really important. I love you just the way you are...and so do the rest of us..."

"I think I'm gonna go for a walk, Windy."

"It's pouring buckets!"

"I feel like going for a walk anyway."

Nicholas sighed. "All right then. I'll have a hot tub and a doctor ready for when you come back with pneumonia..."

Andrew stood in the pouring rain and stared at the façade of the Church of St John the Defender, at the rain-darkened stone and the massive circular stained-glass window above the doors that depicted the church's patron saint wielding a huge two-handed broadsword against forty million barbarians and one very mean-looking something or other that looked to be on a holiday from Hell.

According to Nicholas, the church stood in honour of one Jehan de Grace, a poor farmer who, over two thousand years ago when the City was no more than a cluster of falling-down ramshackle wooden huts, had donned the armour of a fallen knight...whaled the daylights out of an entire army of invaders...and then gone quietly back to his farm to bleed to death of his wounds while whoever was in charge at the time searched high and low for the soldier who had saved his bacon. Legend had it that the his men had found Jehan dead at his plow, so he was buried on the spot...and when the Church had gotten round to being big enough to build churches, and needed people to name them after, one had been erected over the farmer's grave and sanctified in his name.

"He must've been pretty brave," murmured Andrew to himself, "but he couldn't've been very bright to stand up to so many people trying to kill him..."

He pulled his hooded cloak closer around him and turned away towards the Boulevard, with no clear idea where he wanted to go, but content to wander aimlessly until something presented itself to him. When next he looked up from the toes of his boots, the storm had thoroughly soaked him through, and he realised he'd come to the West Abbey Road, not far from Thomas Beverley's flat in Boar's Head Lane. He walked the half block to his friend's door, rang the bell and climbed the two flights of narrow stairs up to Tom's rooms. The writer stood in the glow of an ancient gas-fired lamp at the head of the stairs. his bearish bulk seeming to fill the landing.

"Andrew what in heaven's name are you doing out on a day like this?" demanded Beverley as his friend reached the top of the stairs. "You're drenched, man, and no doubt chilled t'the bone in the bargain. Come on in, y'crazy bastard. Get rid of that cloak. Take your boots off. For God's sake don't worry about dripping all over everywhere...Here! Have a belt of what passes for my poor excuse for brandy while you're at it..."

Andrew allowed himself to be led into the only slightly-controlled chaos of Thomas Beverley's three rooms, eyeing the mounds of papers, books and old magazines that lay scattered over everything. The writer stripped him of his cloak and thrust a somewhat grimy balloon glass of the sub-standard brandy into his chilled hands.

"Good t'see, you, Andy," boomed Thomas, tugging at his shock of brown hair with both paws. "I was needing a break just about now," he went on. "Been working on something that'll scald the hides off those pompous jackasses in the Royal Society, but my quills keep scorching under the strain. Here...sit yourself down on this chair...no...hold on...the chair's over here...under the newspapers...I really ought t'give the place a going over one of these days..."

He straightened up from the excavated armchair and threw a quizzical stare in the direction of his unlooked-for guest.

"You awfully talkative, today, Andrew," he observed a bit more quietly. "No one in their right mind would be out and about wandering in this weather, so I guess there must be something going on in your head. Sit down then...drink the brandy...I'll shut up long enough for you get a word in edgewise. I won't even offer to read you a chapter or seven."

Andrew sat, gulped at the brandy and then coughed for five minutes. When he stopped, and looked up with glistening eyes, Thomas could not have said whether or not the wretched liquor had been responsible.

"Pretty desperate, eh?" he said apologetically. "I'd get some of the better stuff but it would be bad for my image and—"

"Tom, I've got to ask you a question. It's important..."

Beverley sank slowly into the heavy ladder-back wooden chair at his desk, his bantering air switched off as easily as it could be turned on.

"Okay, Andy," he said quietly. "I'm ready. Let's have it."

"D'you think I'm strange because I don't like sleeping with girls as much as boys?"

Thomas stared at him in amazement, his broad face darkening like the thunderclouds that hung over the city.

"Oh hell!" he muttered to himself. "I was afraid this was going t'happen eventually..."

To Andrew he said, "If Windy's done this t'you, Andy, I'm gonna beat him to a bloody pulp—!"

"Tom don't be an idiot of course it wasn't Windy. It was someone else—"

"A first-class bastard whoever it was!"

"I need t'know, Tom...please..."

Beverley sat up straight in his chair and then leaned towards Andrew.

"The short answer is NO," he said without hesitation. "No I don't think you're strange because you like boys better than girls. I can't pretend I understand why you feel that way—and there's no small corner of my soul where I feel sorry I don't because you're a positive joy between the sheets—but no, I don't think you're strange. You're just not like me, that's all. It's the way you are for whatever reasons, and I wouldn't change you for the world...not even for a chance t'get Brandy and Diana all to myself..."

Andrew tugged at his boots and stood up, reaching for his rain-sodden cloak.

"Where're you going now?" Thomas asked, leaping up to bar the door with his massive frame.

Andrew shrugged. "I'm not sure yet, Tom," he said faintly, but with a look of relief beginning to ease the taut misery of his face. "I talked to Windy about it, but I wanted to be sure. Will you tell him I may not be home tonight?"

"You're not gonna do anything stupid, are you, Andy?"

Andrew shook his head and smiled.

"All right then, I'll run over a bit later and tell him," agreed Tom, stepping away from the door. "But you get back to one of us first thing in the morning, right?"

"I will," said Andrew, slipping out onto the landing. "And thank you, Thomas...a lot..."

"Any time, Andy," grinned Beverley. "You know that."

Andrew nodded and went back out into the rain. He thought briefly of going to see Brandywine, who always made him feel better no matter how dreadful anything was, but couldn't bring himself to do it. He had grown ashamed of always seeking her strength when his own failed him.

It was early evening before he came back to the church that stood beside the archway leading into St John's Mews. Much of the storm had blown itself off somewhere else, leaving the City dank and drear in its wake, some streets ankle-deep in rainwater gurgling down into the sewers. Andrew stood on the sidewalk before the church and, after a moment of hesitation, squared his shoulders, flung his cloak back from them and strode through the wrought-iron gates. He climbed the broad stone stairs to the heavy oak doors, that were carved with rosettes and the Cross...and then he went inside...with night and the City itself a million miles away. For a moment his courage failed him as its vast echoing silence swept over him like a tide.

Ranks of empty pews marched away down the length of the nave, almost disappearing in the gloom that flowed down from the clerestory windows above, unrelieved by the timourous glimmer of votive candles that lined the aisles to either side in their cups of amber and crimson glass. Above him, carved faces looked down solemnly from the archways of the nave and triforium arcades; stained glass saints writhed and suffered in silence upon their crosses of pain. The only brightness to reach him came from the altar, where massive tapers stood to a man's height, casting their light upon the huge gilded Cross that seemed to hang suspended in the air above it. And the stillness was so deep and profound that Andrew scarce dared to breathe for fear of it shattering around him. He crept forward, slowly, one step at a time, wincing with each scrape and echo of his boot-heels on the stone floor, until he stood before the altar and there, in desperation, he flung caution away.

"I'm here!" he cried, and his voice shrilled and thundered through the empty church. "I'm here. I'm not a coward!"

When the echoes had fled away into the shadow corners, he heard the whisper of sandaled feet to his right, in the south transept, and Father Ambrosius appeared at the door of one of the small chapels opening onto it.

"So..." he said. "You've come after all."

The faces of stone above them seemed to mime his words endlessly through the murk; when they tired of their sport, silence returned like an invisible wall to stand between the two men...young and old...the priest's face expressionless, like a mask. His voice had evinced neither pleasure nor distaste.

"Yes, sir, I've come after all," said Andrew, forcing the words to come from his lips. "Yesterday afternoon you challenged me. You said I hadn't the courage to stand before your God, to face Him as I am for what I am. Yes, sir, I've come after all. I may be different from you, or what you and yours would condemn as sinful, but I'm no coward."

"Then you remain unrepentant of your sins?" cried Father Ambrosius, walking towards him.

Andrew stood his ground, refused to move as the priest came to glare up into his face.

"Were I to be elsewise, then I would be a denial of everything I am," whispered Andrew. "I've committed no sins, and I'm willing to face your God's judgment at your pleasure, in a manner of your own choosing."

The priest's face softened abruptly, his eyes losing the cold steely glare he had levelled up at the young man.

"My son, I am not a cruel man, nor do I serve a cruel God," he said softly. "His Mercy is boundless. Accept it, I pray you, cast yourself down before Him in His sight and let Him embrace you in His love and forgiveness."

His hands stretched themselves out towards Andrew beseechingly, and a look of compassion overspread his round features.

Andrew shook his head sadly. "I can't do that, Father," he said. "I wouldn't dream of challenging your faith...whatever it is that brings you comfort, makes you who you are. How can you expect it of me?"

Ambrosius let his hands fall helpless to his sides, his face becoming eloquent with sadness.

"So be it," he murmured, making the sign of the Cross between them. I will trust in my God that He will cast his light upon you. Will you stand upon the sacred bones of one who was a defender of the Faith?"

"St John? He fought for his freedom, Father Ambrosius, against those who would have had him and the people of this land bow down to *their* gods and *their* beliefs. I will be no less than John."

"Through this night and on until such time as you have, in some wise, received a judgment?"

"Through a year and a day, if need be," said Andrew.

"Very well," said the priest. "Beneath us lie the mortal remains of he for whom this church was raised, Jehan de Grace, the Defender, who stood between this city and its birth and the hordes of the very Devil himself. It is there I will take you, Master MacKinnon, and it is there you shall await the Word of God...alone...until His voice has been heard."

Andrew nodded his head.

"I'm ready..." he said hoarsely.

The cleric led him along the ambulatory, past the choir, to the rear of the church, where a carved wooden screen stood before a door, and beyond that a flight of winding stairs that went down into the very foundations of the church itself. At the foot of the stairs, a low-vaulted passage hewn from living rock ran back to a place that was directly beneath the altar, and a small wooden door with a steel cross laid into its panels. Ambrosius removed a key from the ring that hung upon the cord at his waist, and unlocked the door.

"Within is the crypt of Jehan de Grace," he said solemnly. "God go with you, and wait upon your Salvation with His infinite patience, as I shall wait upon you here. Each of us shall stand vigil this night."

Andrew nodded wordlessly and passed through the doorway, heard it close behind him and the key turn again in its lock. He was alone in the crypt, even as Ambrosius had promised.

It was a small rectangular place of light grey stone, its walls hidden for the most part by arrases of white samite cloth embroidered with crimson crosses, save where sconced candles were lit to dispel what would have been total darkness. Beneath the farthest wall was a slab of stone marked with yet another cross, and standing over it was the statue of a mailed and armoured knight, with a great stone broadsword held rood-like in his gloved hands. Here it was that the sainted body of Jehan de Grace...John the Defender...lay in its eternal rest. Here the silence was much different from that which had filled the church above; here it was the silence of the grave... and something else that was deep and powerful and ineffably holy.

He didn't know what to do or say, but stood with his back to the door, with his cloak still dripping at whiles upon the bare stone floor beneath his feet. At length he took it off, and the plain coat he wore beneath it, now standing in his shirt and trousers, dark hair clinging damply to the drawn and suddenly haggard lineaments of his face. Impulsively, he strode across the floor and knelt before the stone of the crypt itself, bowing his head over clasped hands.

"I don't know what I'm supposed t'do." he said aloud. "I don't know the proper way to say prayers, or even if I must pray at all. It seems I've always been as I am now, and thought my thoughts without ever wondering if anyone else would ever hear them. If you are God—-or one of them, as Windy says—then you must know why I'm here and you

know my thoughts, my prayers, the words in my poems that are just me. Ambrosius says I have sinned but I don't believe him..."

And that was the end of it, the sum and the total of why Andrew had come. Had his life depended upon it he could not have said anything more, so he became silent within the silence of the crypt, knelt there upon the stone, waiting for something...anything...that might pass for an answer to whatever the question had been...

Time went on timelessly. Second to second. Minute to minute. Breath to each halting breath. Until the seconds and minutes became hours, and Andrew's breathing became slow and measured to match the passage of Time, and in the heartbeat of the Universe he was lost in the pounding of his own heart, beating with fear and desperate Hope.

His knees began to ache with the burden of his weight upon them, and then the pain went away, only to return again...and depart a second time...and a third...and a fourth...until it seemed to him that he had never been aught else but a small child buried beneath the earth, waiting for a word of Love.

He dozed and waked a dozen times, but that was long after thirst and hunger had made him faint and light-headed, so that he could not distinguish between either state.

Somewhere in the midst of this half-dreaming, a flickering of light upon the walls made him look up, and he saw the candles guttering in their sconces on the walls. Suddenly, he felt the stone shudder beneath him, and a low ponderous rumbling disturb the utter stillness. The candles writhed in their death agonies, casting shadows where no shadows ought to be; a breath of ghost-wind ruffled the draperies of the crypt...and then a pale ghost-light came into being above him as the candles flared once and died. Andrew came awake, his eyes starting from their sockets, the spectral light now spreading over the entirety of the vaulted ceiling, creeping down the walls, across the floor...

The low rumbling became stronger, as if the bones of the earth were being ground together by a titan's hands, raging with passion, burgeoning into a thunder that filled the crypt, deafening his ears, as the light hemmed him round the stone slab and grew to blinding brilliance as it crept over him...swallowed him whole...

Andrew closed his eyes, clenched his teeth together and wept as the floor fell away from beneath him, dizzy as the rending and crashing of the world pounded into his head and absolute terror shrieked in his soul. It became unbearable and went on to become something immeasurably worse...the dissolution of Self...

Andrew screamed with fear and revelation. An explosion of sound rocked the church above him, shattered the door at his back...and when he felt that Death now had surely come to claim him for his sins, there was suddenly a sense of incomparable Peace, and he felt the touch of lips upon his own...

THE UNFADNG FLOWER

Ambrosius dragged himself up from the stone floor of the passage, staggered forward through the splinters of the door that had closed upon the crypt, stared in wonder at the sight before him. His lips moved in a silent prayer, his hands moved in the sign of the Cross, over and over again as the brilliant light that had sheared its way through the broken door and the darkness slowly faded away, and candle-flame leapt up again from the wall-sconces.

On trembling legs that threatened to give way beneath him, he went to the pale figure who lay upon the riven stone of the crypt, gathered him up and cried out to see the last of the ghost-light lingering upon the face of the unconscious boy he held in his arms. And when finally he looked up at the stone effigy of Jehan de Grace, he saw that the stone broadsword now lay in shards at its feet...and beneath those shards...etched into the new foundation of his faith...were the words...

Quamdiu ibi est Amor
As long as there is Love

The Artlessness of Loving

for Kaiine

Somewhere well along in the month of November when the City occasionally could be said to be afflicted with *gloomy* weather, someone forgot to tell whoever was in charge. The last few days of the month suddenly became glorious with sunshine that brought an unseasonal *warmth* as well as light; in celebration, people went about in shirt sleeves and summer dresses, and the cafes all along the Boulevard liberated terrace furnishings only just relegated to their winter homes in cellars and storage sheds.

On the second such morning, Windy decided a day-long stroll was in order. He measured his morning coffee in gulps rather than leisurely sips, dressing in short bursts that had him back and forth between his bedroom closet and the windows in his music room, there to watch the play of the light—and a frisky band of felines—on the cobblestones of his courtyard. Not long after, in a light linen suit he usually wore with the springtide, he strode out into the morning with a jaunty step and a pocketful of treats to offer up to the furry four-foots along his way. Halfway to the church at the end of the laneway he direct encountered his neighbour, once again camped beside his own front door, slashing away at a half-finished canvas.

"G'morning, Robertson."

'Morning t'you, Nicholas," he replied. "Quite the day. If it keeps up they'll have to re-open all the beaches and make up new names for the months that used t'be winter."

He stood up and stretched, a tall stocky figure with a shock of salt-and-pepper hair, in canvas trousers and a work-shirt rolled up at the sleeves along surprisingly-muscled forearms. A pair of piercing blue eyes gleamed out from his rather blunt features; he seemed to be measuring Windy for something, but was not quite ready to acknowledge it to either of them.

"Heard Ambrosius got his hooks into that young friend of yours a while back," he said by way of avoiding the issue. "That pale dark-haired fellow, how's he doing?"

"Andy? Andy's doing fine. Took him a while to get his feet back under him, but for all one might be ready to climb all over Ambrosius for being an holier-than-thou fool, I think they both learned something to their betterment that night."

"Robertson nodded. "Well...so long as the young one is all right. Ambrosius has his precious God to look after *him*."

Now it was Windy's turn to change the direction of their conversation.

"Haven't seen *you* out and about in a while," he said.

Robertson shrugged. "Been working pretty steady at something...ever since that night you set the whole place to rumbling."

"Not this one here..." said Windy, nodding towards the canvas beside the door.

"No no...d'you remember the one I was trying to start up that night...that bit about painting in the moonlight? Well... bit by bit whatever it was I was trying t'do sort of worked itself out."

"Glad to hear that," grinned Nicholas. "But it's a bit strange, Robertson. We've been neighbours for what...maybe three years now...but it's only recently I've begun to notice your paintings almost everywhere I go. House parties and a lot of the galleries. You're fairly well thought of."

Robertson shrugged again. "For what that's worth. Besides, they're all old hat, my friend. Nowadays I'm in it just for myself. People keep asking me for paintings, but I'm not really interested anymore."

"Well you should be," Windy said earnestly. "I'm not surprised t'find you as good as you are, just surprised it took me so long to find out. Sometimes when I look at your work I feel like I should be able to step right into them, or there's something or someone in there half a glimpse away from me noticing them."

Robertson looked a bit embarrassed.

"I don't take compliments that well," he growled, "but I will from you. On account of the wee blonde thing keeps comin' round t'see you."

"You mean Brandy?" asked Nicholas.

"If that's her name, then aye, she's the one," nodded the painter. "I've been around a long while," he said softly, almost to himself. "Longer than I ever thought t'be...longer than I ever cared t'be...but I imagine I've forgotten a lot of things I used t'know. Maybe your Brandy girl showed me one of 'em, but I was out here one evening cursin' and swearin' and along she comes to look over my shoulder and then apologises for being so forward; then, like she was reading my mind, she tells me if I want this kind of shadow I should go with something a tad darker, with some of this that or the other mixed in...and sure enough, I get my shadow spot on. I was a bit stunned to be takin' instruction from a girl that young, but I managed to thank her, got over myself when she smiled..."

Windy smiled too. "Branny's a lot better than she thinks she is," he said. "She can carry a colour in her head for weeks and then match it to anything. And there's nothing in the world better than when she smiles."

Robertson looked thoughtful again, his face taking on that measuring look.

"I'm fairly certain we've crossed paths before...but listen, Nicholas," he said slowly. "Not just now, but soon, I'd like t'show you something. Get your opinion. The painting I was trying for that other night."

"So you did finish it!" said Windy.

"I don't know," said Robertson. "That's why I want you t'see it...and there's a story t'go with so I don't know if it's your opinion I want so much as maybe just someone t'listen while I talk."

"I'd be honoured," said Wyndham.

Robertson snorted. "Get on with ya," he said. "I'll catch you up one o' these days..."

One of these days was about a week later, when the weather had gone back to the more "normal" raw and drooky, and most everyone in the City came close to sighs of relief that things were back as they were expected to be; but on the next day, when they all were yet revelling in the warmth, Nicholas found Brandy camped beside the canal, her face wreathed in honey-blonde curls a study in fierce concentration as she strove to recreate sunlight bouncing off the water on a good-sized frame of canvas.

"Windy," she said…smiling…but breathlessly, as if the effort had been a bit much. "Wow am I ever so glad to see you! Thank you for rescuing me. I don't think I'm managing this very well today, and I don't know if it's worth the effort if what's here today is gone tomorrow, or the sun is doing things different from what it's doing now."

Nicholas made helpless noises and suggested that some things looked after themselves and maybe today the sun didn't want anyone making sport with its water-bouncing. Brandy looked relieved.

"You know, I think you might be right," she sighed. "I guess I'm just going to have to figure out another way…but what am I supposed t'do until I *do* figure it out?

She pouted. Windy felt his knees go a bit weak.

"Maybe we could talk about it at the Silver Rose?" he suggested, and sat down on the bench beside her.

She was delightfully *gaminesque* in baggy old corduroy trousers and a raggedy thin white dress shirt covered in paint spatters and smooshes much like the big one of chrome yellow that adorned her right cheek.

"Could we?" she cried earnestly. "That would be so nice."

She smiled a smile that put the afternoon light to shame and he was grateful to be sitting down. After a minute or so he helped her pack up her paint-box, canvas and easel, shouldered all of it, and they staggered off arm-in-arm.

"I have enough for a glass of that wonderful May wine and maybe a sweet," she said.

"I've enough for whatever you'd like, and I invited you so it's my treat."

"But you always pay, Windy...it doesn't seem fair."

He got that weak feeling again, but borrowed some fortitude from an arm around her shoulders.

"Brandy, you and the rest of our friends are my family now, and as I've been lucky enough to have come from better *circumstances*, I have to look out for all of you. I don't mind at all, and I don't care about the money. I just want us all to be happy together."

She became sad.

"I'm sorry you don't have anyone," she said softly.

"But I do!" he said. "My parents are still alive, and I've got three *older* brothers. I've not been treated badly, but I think my brothers all feel a bit relieved I'm here, so there's one less of us while they jostle about for who gets to run the works back home. I'm rewarded on a monthly basis for *not* being involved."

"That sounds terrible," she said.

"Not at all. I'm quite happy with the arrangement. What about you then?" he asked.

She leaned against him, put her head down against his chest.

"I don't have anyone but you and Andy and Gareth and Di and Thomas," she whispered.

"I'm a foundling. A doorstep bundle."

"Well maybe that's what you were, but it's not what you are now," he said earnestly. "Now you're the prettiest member of the *Boulevardiers*, a ragtag association of whatever we are, bent on mischief and mayhem."

"Oh don't let Diana hear you!" she cried. "We've always been friends, but sometimes I think she doesn't really like me very much at all."

"That's not true, Brandywine Lloyd," he said, and it was indeed the truth that *he* spoke. Early on there had been a night when they all had staggered about somewhat less than soberly, and Diana had ended up in his bed when everyone else had fallen asleep downstairs.

"I wish I could be more like her," she'd said wistfully, *"instead of getting all huffy over things that don't quite suit me whenever. Brandy's not got a cruel bone in her body. It's like nothing bad can ever change her from what she's always been from the moment she opened her eyes..."*

"How d'you know that?"

"I just do, Branny. I just do."

She put her arms around his waist a bit more tightly and sighed.

"I hope you're right. She's so beautiful and elegant and—"

"And every bit as impressed by you as you are by her..."

At the Silver Rose they sat on the terrace and waved at everyone who passed by on the Boulevard. Brandy ordered a strawberry tart and drank May wine, and was thoroughly scandalised when their waiter, who knew them quite well and whose name was Armando, grinned and asked if *Madamoiselle*

wished to be rid of the smudge of paint on her cheek at the same time he removed the whipped cream from the tip of her nose.

"You never said!" she cried to Nicholas a moment later. "I'm so embarrassed. You big poophead why didn't tell me?"

Nicholas had been drinking brandy from a balloon glass whilst drinking Brandy with his eyes. He *tried* to look apologetic.

"I thought it looked nice," he said, somewhat woozily. "You *are* an artist, after all, and it was a very becoming paint smudge."

She punched him in the arm but without too much enthusiasm.

"You're still a poophead," she said.

"And you're a very talented artist. I was talking to Robertson just yesterday and he confirmed my suspicions."

She looked incredulous. Then she looked terrified. Nicholas had to concentrate.

"Honestly. He said he was outside his door one day when you came by and you gave him some advice about something he was working on that was perfect."

"He was just being polite I—"

"No Branny he meant it...every word...and as I was walking off I heard him say something like *She looks so much like her...*"

Brandywine's eyes got big.

"He said something like that to me too! What did he mean?"

"I have no idea," said Nicholas, "but I think we need one more glass each and then maybe we should think about how we're going t'get home without the *gendarmerie* offering us accommodations for the night..."

So the weather changed, went back to being almost-winter. The terrace furniture disappeared back into the cellars, overcoats and scarves replaced linen suits and sun dresses. Windy stayed close to home, and realised he was waiting...until late one afternoon he saw Robertson coming across their the courtyard, favouring his right leg as he limped to Windy's door, knocked quietly and stood outside in the chill, waiting for Nicholas to invite him in.

In answer to Wyndham's unspoken question, Robertson glanced down at his leg and raised up his hand as if to say *Wait...I'll explain soon enough...* They went into the front parlour, where a wood fire crackled and sputtered on the hearth.

Windy poured them each a glass of whiskey from an heavy crystal decanter and they sat down in two armchairs, sheltering in the shadows just outside the glow of the fire. For a while they sat in silence with their glasses. Robertson drew a deep breath...

Aengus Robertson's Story

"I was born a long time ago, just north o' the Carillon valley outside a place called Glen Carrick, a small village tucked alongside one of the mountain streams that feed the—"

"Findhorn," said Windy softly. "I grew up in the Carillon...spent a lot of summers fishing with my brothers at a spot not far from Glen Carrick."

Robertson thrust his face forward, his head to one side, peering at him from under his brows.

"You're one o' the *Carillon* Wyndhams?" he asked incredulously.

Nicholas nodded.

"My story is before your time, but maybe you know some of it without the tellin'," said Robertson. "D'you know of the *de Montenays*, as well?"

"Of course. My father used t'grind his teeth whenever he'd come up against a bit of his history with old Dorion de Montenay."

Robertson wagged his head in something somewhere between total disbelief and the unlooked-for serendipity of disparate lives coming together out of nowhere. He reached for Windy's decanter of whisky and poured them both another generous round. As if to lend some theatre to the strangeness of coincidence, an harbinger of winter wind swept over the cobbled courtyard outside, whistled outside the windows of the sitting room and then plunged down the chimney, setting the flames on the hearth to a good measure of mad dancing. Robertson shivered, began again...

"I was the eldest of seven children, all of them girls but me" he said, staring at the fire through the gold in his glass. "My father was the local blacksmith and I was his pride and joy, growing taller and stronger even than he himself, standing hours alongside him at the forge, and when come of age, matching him glass for glass at the pub.

"We were poor by most standards, but proud beyond measure, our family having served the first King Michael de Montigny in the Northland Wars, and even winning from him the haft and point of a spear he'd broken in battle when the Scandians came brawling down over the mountains.

"So I sweated by day and strutted by night. I could do no wrong in my father's eyes, and what kind of young man can ask for anything better than that. Only perhaps that while the bed in my father's house was more often than not empty, it was because I was out prowling the countryside and takin' my pleasure with every man's daughters wherever we could find a braeside in the summer, or the hayloft in a barn by winter. And then

...then..."

He stopped, raised up his glass in one sharp motion, tossed his head back and emptied it in a single draught. Nicholas saw tears glistening in the firelight, that squeezed themselves out from his closed eyes, and waited in the silence while Robertson put his head down and tried half a dozen times to go on. He filled Robertson's glass for a third time...

"One day in the spring of my twentieth year, she came through Glen Carrick on a great bay gelding thrown a shoe as they come down the vale from the manor house above the village. Somehow I'd never laid eyes on her before, and I'd never seen anyone like her. She was sunshine in the rich velvet and leather of a highborn, and the only way I can describe her to you would be t'say that she and your Brandy might have been birth-sisters, and I fell in love with her in an instant."

Again he stopped, shook his head as if shake away the cobwebs upon his memory, that he might see her again so clearly as he had seen her then.

"There was nothing about her from her father. Her brown eyes shone with a light of such generosity as to stun you speechless where you stood; her voice was soft and full of so much kindness as to make you weep for some desperate ill luck

56

to befall you that she might bestow it upon you in sympathy. She begged my assistance, not for herself, but to be certain her horse had come to no harm. I handed her down from her saddle, made her a place to sit outside the forge, with a mug of water to drink while she waited. I told her my name, and she told me hers...Rochelle de Montenay...Dorion de Montenay's own firstborn daughter..."

He stared down into his glass, seemed to regard it as something never before encountered, before raising it slowly to his lips and taking only the smallest most reverent sip of the whiskey, where before he had dashed it down entire.

"I don't need to tell what likely you know well enough; that in the same time that my family served the first king in battle against the Scandians, there was a younger-by-one-year brother to Michael who felt his claim to the newly-made newly-saved Amaranth Throne was as good as his older brother's; that there in the aftermath of the slaughter gave birth to our country, they looked at each other and Reginald was compelled to bend his knee to Michael and give up the name of *de Montigny* forever. On that day he became Reginald de Montenay, and never once set foot in the palace raised up to house his brother's dynasty...and never once forgot that day...nor ever let his children or his children's children forget that they too, were of this land's royal blood. There was talk of talismans and magic, and the de Montigny kings always seemed to outlive the lives and enmity of the de Montenays. Dorion was no different from any of his forebears. They ruled our corner of the world as if it belonged to them, never so harshly as to attract anyone's attention, but always with their noses stuck up in the air just that wee bit higher than those of their neighbours...

"And then I found Rochelle and she found me...and in time we were discovered, of course. Our world was no so great that we could escape anyone's notice, never mind that of her father. Dorion forbid her to see me ever again, locked her in her rooms, set watch over her every waking hour...and still there were those in the household who loved their lord's daughter better than they loved him, and saw to it that we should have our time together."

Robertson set his glass aside, and now to Windy's eyes there was no doubt of his grief, nor any attempt to hide his tears.

"One murderous overcast night we were discovered together, by her father and a dozen of his men. They hounded us out from our trysting place and we fled away down along the banks of our stream to where it plunged down a hundred feet to the plains below. It was pitch dark as we ran above the falls. Neither one of us was much more than blind with fear and desperation. Neither one of us could move quickly enough when the cliffside fell apart beneath our feet and we went down...

"We fell for what felt like forever, hand in hand until we hit the water below and I felt my right leg shatter on the rocks...I heard her scream...and as if to mock us the moon come out from behind its pall of clouds so I could watch the flood carry her away..."

Robertson wept openly, and when Nicholas set his own glass aside, struck so much with the horror and the image of that night that he leapt forward to catch him up in his arms as he fell from his chair, he found that he wept as well...and so they crouched there together upon the floor before his hearth as if the world had come to an end around them and there was nothing left for either of them but the Void itself.

"...I was in the water for days, aware only of the pain, barely conscious at the best of times, always praying for no consciousness at all. Somewhere along the way, far enough from Glen Carrick that news of *the laird's loss* never reached them, strangers pulled me out and found someone to do what they could for my leg.

"When I could move again I came here, as far away as I could go from my village. I never saw my family again, never made any attempt to let them know I had survived, because then I might have had to deal with their concern and their love, when all I wanted was my Rochelle...

"Much later, I learned that she had gone without a trace; that her father had spent months along the riverbanks, questioning anyone who might have seen either of us, found her as the farmers had found me. He died five years later, but not before he made life a livin' hell for everyone around him....and I...I became a famous artist and scarcely lived at all until your beautiful friend stopped to offer me some advice about shadows."

He became silent. Again they sat before Windy's fire while the wind outside howled derision at them, battered at the diamond panes and blew down the chimney to scatter sparks at their feet. Nicholas poured the last of the whisky. Robertson looked up at him, bleary-eyed with drink and the reborn memory of pain and loss.

"And that's my tale," he whispered. "All y'need t'know. All there is, but for the painting..."

He rose up from his chair, limped slowly to the front door, awkwardly shrugged into his coat.

"Robertson, surely it can wait for the morning."

Robertson looked down at his boots, unmoving save for the slightest shake of his head.

"Now," he said hoarsely. "Please..."

So Windy took him by the arm and they lurched out into the wind and across the courtyard until they came to Robertson's door. Inside he seemed suddenly to have become so ancient it was a wonder to Nicholas that he could stand at all. Robertson lit an oil lamp and took him through his darkened rooms into one that smelled of paint and turpentine, high-windowed from the north, where the walls were covered with unframed canvases and the floors nearly impassable for the lean of still more against the wainscoting.

In the centre of the room was a shrouded easel. Robertson said nothing, but stripped away the shroud, and Windy stood before a six-foot high canvas that blazed out into the semi-darkness of the room, chasing away the shadows as if a newborn sun had risen of itself up from the stone floor.

"Robertson, what is it?" asked Windy. "It *looks* like when you might stare up into the sun for a moment, on a day when it's so hot you can see the heat coming off of it in waves as it fills the sky."

"I don't know what it is, Nicholas," was his reply, "but to find it I listened every night for the breath and song of this city, as it came to all of us on that one night...and with your girl's help I found the background that made the light seem to jump at us...

"I don't know what it is, but it's almost exactly what I saw in front of my eyes in the days and nights after I lost Rochelle...on the river...when I knew in my heart that she was gone and I prayed to die..."

Windy helped Robertson to bed, already half asleep himself. In the days that followed, the Wheel turned well into Winter and mostly he kept to himself. Haunted by another man's sorrow and loss, he composed a requiem for a girl he'd never known, hoping it might ease Robertson's pain; but almost a fortnight went by with not a word from his neighbour and one evening in twilight Brandywine came to visit him, and remarked that no lights shone in the house where Robertson lived.

The door was unlocked. There was nothing but total darkness as they inched their way together through each room...until they came to Robertson's studio and there they found light in a thin stream beneath the door...knocked once and then cautiously let themselves in. The canvas stormed at them, blinding coruscations of light that the canvas itself seemed barely able to contain.

"He's not here," said Brandy.

"No," said Windy. "I think you're right. He's not here at all."

Shielding his eyes he knelt before the canvas and came away with a folded scrap of paper that he found beneath a small pile of clothing.

I've gone to find her was all it said.

Of Silver Stars & a Siren Singing

for Sterling

Thomas Beverley consulted the somewhat mangled remains of the small white business card he held in one gloved hand, checked the address on it and then, with no small amount of disappointment, eyed the corresponding number over the door of a dingy sub-street level storefront. The business card had come into his possession wholly by chance—he had found it in a mound of snow on the Boulevard—and he had spent the better part of two days trying to locate the shop, wandering back and forth among the narrow lanes of the harbour-front until a grizzled old sailor happened to point him in the right direction.

Now he stood before the object of his quest, his bearlike figure muffled in a greatcoat against the light but persistent fall of sleet and snow that had made his search a chilly one—an interminable slog through the coldest, dampest, and generally rottenest March the City had seen in years. He gazed upon the grime-streaked windows below him—filled with tattered books in tattered dust wrappers, and all manner of things that now seemed to pass as collectable—and cast a distrustful eye upon the short flight of icebound steps leading down to the door of the shop. Then he shook himself once, dislodging a mantle of very wet snow from his shoulders, and threw caution to the winds.

"You've not played cat and mouse with all sorts of winter plagues and pestilence to funk over a half dozen slippery stairs," he said to himself, taking a firm hold on the rusty iron rail that hung beside the stairs. "Who knows if what you're looking for is lurking down there, and the worst can happen is you won't find anything worth buying."

He placed one booted foot gingerly down upon the first step and descended into the snow-filled well before the door, turned the knob and entered the shop to the deafening clang of a large bell attached to it and the doorframe. A rush of warmth enveloped him at once, and as he stood on the doormat stamping the snow from his boots, a tall thoroughly bizarre-looking figure strode noiselessly through a curtained archway at the rear of the shop and impaled him with a glance from one monocled eye.

"Whattayawant?" barked the proprietor of the shop. "And watch where you kick all that damned white stuff I just had the carpets cleaned!"

Beverley scarce knew what to say or where to direct his attention first. Briefly he entertained the notion of informing the shopkeeper that there were no carpets on his floor, but thought better of that immediately; instead he let his gaze wander over the lunatic clutter of all the things that had ever escaped from the attics of ancient homes—books, faded picture postcards in bulging shoeboxes, gilded scrollwork lamps with no shades, and porcelain figurines long past shiny new and now in danger of becoming splintery 3-D jigsaw puzzles where they perched precariously on their shelves. On the other hand, the rather abrupt gentleman who had greeted him so warmly was every bit as picturesque.

He had come through the archway in what could only be described as an "aged bookseller's shuffle", yet now he stood ramrod straight, two inches taller than Thomas' own six-feet, and glared at him from under a pair of shaggy silvered brows that matched the impeccably barbered crown of hair on his head. A pencil-thin brigadier's moustache adorned his upper lip, curled slightly in a scornful welcome, and he wore an elegant embroidered dressing gown of Oriental origin over a pair of truly ragged flannel trousers, and house slippers with upward-pointy toes.

"Well...?" he demanded. "Are you going to just stand there all day wasting my time, or do you have a reason for barging in here and mucking up my floors?"

Thomas blinked, unwound the green-and-white scarf about his neck and consulted the business card in his hand a second time.

"Is this the Edmund Chilton Second Hand and Rare Everything Emporium?" he asked slowly, reading from the card.

"What of it?" growled the man, taking a step towards him and again spearing him with his monocled eye. "You don't like what you see, get out..."

Thomas gave him a wary look and drew a deep breath.

"I need help—"

"I can see that," interrupted the shopkeeper, "but if you're here looking for paperbound romances at half price, you can start whistling...and where in Heaven's name did you get that scarf? The last time I saw anything that awful was...well...never mind when it was...either state your business or be on your way, young fellow. I'm not giving anything away, including the heat..."

Beverley remained rooted on the doormat and stared at the proprietor as if scalded by all the heat not being given away. Most of the booksellers in the City knew him quite well and went out of their way to be helpful, even though they were well aware of his limited means; this fellow, however, seemed intent upon insulting him straight out the door, and while Thomas could live with that as easily as not, it was the uniqueness of his approach to bookselling that left him somewhat at a loss for words.

"I'm looking for a book," he said finally, enunciating each word with care as he sought to reassemble the shards of his composure.

The man withdrew the painful aspect of his glare and grinned amiably.

"I certainly hope so," he said cheerily. "Else I can't imagine why you'd put up with my welcome. In any case, I'm Edmund Chilton and now since you're here, come on in, make yourself comfortable and we can talk some turkey...and for God's sake get your chin off the floor before you pickle it in the road-salt you've tromped in."

Thomas closed his mouth with a snap and tried to visually map a route through the chaos of this and that littering the floor of the shop. It wasn't a difficult task; one quick survey was enough to reassure him that the place was very much like his own digs in Boar's Head Lane. Chilton watched him for a moment, shook his head and then flung himself into a leather-backed swivel chair behind a desk hidden at the rear of the shop. He picked up a stinky old brier, fired it into a volcanic gush of aromatic smoke and smiled up at his customer.

"What can I do for you?" he inquired briskly.

Thomas removed his gloves and negotiated the particularly dangerous stretch of floor space that passed between a dilapidated old hobby horse and a stack of old magazines that threatened to pitch itself over, avalanche-wise, onto his head.

"I'm trying to locate a book called—"

Chilton shot a manicured finger up at him and his eyes narrowed dangerously.

"Let's get one thing straight before we go on," he said wearily. "Books have titles. *Call* them what you like on your own time, but in here books have proper *titles* and don't you forget it."

Thomas ran a hand through his hair and inspected the cobwebs on the ceiling where it joined the wall at Chilton's back, thinking to himself, *I must be going mad. He's right, of course, books have titles...one doesn't call them anything...but that hardly seems a good enough excuse not to strangle the old bastard.*

He left off studying the cobwebs and returned his gaze to the bookseller, who grinned at him with an almost devilish glint in his monocled eye before winking with the other.

"Now...what was the *title* of the book you were looking for?" he said, arching a feathery white eyebrow.

"*Of Silver Stars and a Siren Singing*," Thomas replied carefully. "By Jefferson Lancaster Monday. It's horribly rare—"

"You're darn tootin' it's rare," interrupted Chilton, levelling a pipe-stem at Beverley. "Which is why I'm going t'soak you for it when it comes time to reckon our account."

Thomas gawped at him in amazement.

"You've got a copy...*Of Silver Stars and a Siren Singing*...by Jefferson Lancaster Monday...Peacock Press...Bombay and Baltimore...1876...in cornflower cloth with silver stamping...?!?!?!?!"

"Limited to five hundred copies with twelve tipped-in colour plates by the author."

"That's the one," breathed Thomas. "My God. You have one...?

"Have I ever lied to you?" asked the bookseller innocently.

"You really *really* have a copy?"

"I do...but I'm afraid it's signed by Monday on the title page," Chilton smiled benignly.

"Fourth case from the window on the wall to my right, third shelf down, ninth book from the left."

Beverley stared at him incredulously for an instant, before turning and trying to make his way to the bookcase in question without trampling and tripping over everything else in his path. Once there he did the requisite counting three shelves down, nine books from the left, and found it just where it was supposed to be. He retraced his steps with the book clutched in his trembling hands, and found Chilton puffing serenely on his pipe.

"This is it! Oh my God...it's...it's..."

"A mint copy," finished the bookseller smugly. "Never been read. Some of the pages are still uncut."

"It's worth a fortune."

"It's worth a couple of thousand easy, Mister...ah...?"

"Beverley. Thomas Beverley. D'you know how long I've been looking for this book?"

"Certainly nowhere near as long as I've owned it," grinned Chilton. "Pony up, lad, I've got a business to run here."

"I don't have anywhere near a couple of thousand to pay you for it," said Thomas. "I don't have anywhere near a couple of hundred..."

"How about fifty bucks? If that's too much you can take a hike."

"But it's thievery. You'll have me arrested the minute I walk out the door! This book—"

"Is gonna cost you fifty big ones, Beverley," snapped Chilton impatiently. If you don't like the price—"

"I know. I can take a hike."

"My but you're a quick study."

Thomas did some rapid calculations in his head and came to the unalterable conclusion that if he paid fifty dollars for the book, his next month's rent payment would leave him within a sneeze of total bankruptcy. He gazed down at the volume still in his hands, marvelled at its newness, the delicious silken feel of the cloth...the untarnished silver stamping. He looked up at the book seller, afraid the old bugger had been leading him on just to amuse himself.

"Will you take a cheque?" he asked.

"With forty-two pieces of identification, your blood type *and* your mother's maiden name. Used to ask for firstborn sons, but I noticed business slacked off too much even for *my* liking."

"How about my word that the cheque is good?" Thomas snapped, and then cringed inwardly when it came out sounding huffy as hell. Chilton grinned.

"Oh...so there's some fire in your blood after all, is there? I was beginning to wonder, you know. Not many people would've put up with me for as long as you have and—"

"Will you take my cheque or not?"

The monocle dropped from the bookseller's eye as both went wide with delight; then he picked up a fountain pen and tossed it across his desk.

"Sold," he said with a smile. "You write while I wrap."

Thomas allowed the book to be pried from his fingers and watched the man disappear with it into the back room of the shop. He was waving the cheque in the air, waiting for the ink to dry, when Chilton reappeared with the book in a neat parcel of brown paper.

Their hands met in mid-air over the desk, book and cheque changing ownership.

"Thank you...very much," Thomas said stiffly. "It's been a pleasure doing business with you."

Chilton laughed. "Don't be ridiculous," he said, "I've been abrupt and unconscionably rude and I really owe you an apology...though if I were you I wouldn't hold my breath waiting for it."

"Well thanks anyway," replied Thomas, figuring the admission was a close as he was going to get. "I've got Monday's other three books, but this one...finally...you have no idea what this means..."

"That's for sure," affirmed the bookseller, "though I've got a sneaking suspicion that it means you're going to have to read it on an empty stomach."

Thomas shot him an incredulous stare, but Chilton's face became an inscrutable mask.

"Well...whether you know it or not, you've done me an immeasurable service today," he said, trying for a conciliatory tone. "I shall be forever in your debt."

"The hell you will!" exploded the bookseller suddenly. "Back here day and night trying to make it up to me? I don't think so! I've got your cheque and you've got my book. We're even. All square. Now shove off and let me get back to whatever it was I was doing when you blew in here."

Beverley tucked the parcel under his greatcoat and decided to take the man at his word, before he was offered another more irresistible urge to strangle him. He turned on his heels, inched his way back to the door of the shop and slammed it behind him as he left.

When he was gone the bookseller shook his head, resumed his seat behind the desk and re-fired his brier. A moment later the curtain at his back rustled ever so slightly and a huge marmalade cat with huge green eyes vaulted onto his lap, purring to beat the band. Chilton scratched one tufted ear affectionately.

"I must be getting old, Samantha," he said mock-sorrowfully. "In the old days I never would have given him a chance to catch his breath, much less get in a few words of his own. And the fellow even had me inches from apologising...!

"However...it's no concern of yours, my little beauty, though I'm grateful for the heads-up. I was fairly certain he was one of that ragtag bunch...

"Come on, then, my girl. We've done our deed for the day. Maybe this one will do the trick for him. Meanwhile, let's get you some dinner and then I think I'd better start practising my snarls again...."

The cat blinked once and headed for the back room. Chilton stood up and followed her, but not before he tore the cheque in his hand into four rectangles and laid them neatly on his desk.

Thomas stopped at the Dragon's Jaws on his way home, wedged himself into a corner of the smoke-filled tavern, ordered a rum toddy to drive out the chill of his walk across the City and, at the same time, celebrate the imminence of his insolvency. As he waited for his mug to arrive, he carefully took the brown-papered parcel from beneath his greatcoat and set it on the table before him, not daring to open it though the temptation to do so was overwhelming. He still had a fair bit of trudging to do before he reached his flat, and the weather promised to get worse before it ever began to get better. He contented himself by staring at the featureless paper, imagining what was held therein, and began to run through his prospects for the acquisition of funds in the near future.

I must have been out of my mind to buy that damn thing, he berated himself. *But how could I not? He was giving it away...a signed copy! I suppose I can always borrow a few bits from Windy if things get too tight; then again, perhaps the Weekly will take another pair of articles if I plead poverty and promise not to slang the council too hard...*

His musings were interrupted by the arrival of his toddy and a cry of greeting from one of the many writers who frequented the Jaws. Thomas looked up, nodded in reply and, with a careless wag of his head, invited the newcomer to join him.

"Beverley you old scoundrel how are you?"

Thomas waited patiently as Philip Johnstone went through the unvarying ritual of divesting himself of his muffler, coat and sweater, a process that never took less than three minutes but no more than four. When all his outerwear was folded neatly over the back of a chair, he signed to the barman for his usual and a second toddy for Thomas.

"They're on me, old sod," he said with a grin. "Just got word in today's post. The Clarendon Press is taking my volume of essays...and paying me in the bargain! Five hundred, can you believe it? If the place wasn't so crowded with bottomless pits masquerading as writers I'd stand the house."

Thomas made congratulatory noises, thanked Johnstone for his largesse, and fell to communing silently with the yellow splotch of butter on the surface of the toddy.

"So...how are things going with that novel, Tom? You're about due for your share of the pie."

"I certainly hope so," swore Thomas fervently, edging away from the fact that his novel was moving along at a pace that might have been mistaken for standing still. Instead, he went on to relate the detail of his purchase and cocked his head towards the parcel on the table.

"You paid that much for one book?" said Johnstone incredulously. "You've gone crazed right round the bend..."

"No doubt," growled Thomas, "but now I've got all four of Monday's books—"

"And will likely starve to death before you get to read this last one!"

Beverley shrugged. "The first one sat for almost three months before I got to it, but once it was gone I went through the next pair as soon as I laid hands on them."

Johnstone looked impressed.

"This Monday character must be one hell of a writer," he observed. "You don't do much more than sneer at most books. What's he about…?"

"Like nothing you've ever read, I'll wager," said Thomas. "For that matter, he's like nothing I've ever read either, and the devil knows why I like him. This one's cal…titled *Of Silver Stars & a Siren Singing*, and if it's anything like the others it's filled with magic, mythical monsters and at least one incomparably beautiful woman."

"You've got t'be joking. You don't read that sort of tripe."

"I know," nodded Thomas," yet there's something about Monday that fascinates me…but listen, Johnstone, apart from my penchant for writing and reading the most depressing things imaginable, you know most of the booksellers in the City. What about the fellow who sold me *Silver Stars*, this Edmund Chilton? He's got a tatty old shop down by the docks…in Bedford Street…"

Whisky and Thomas' second toddy arrived. Johnstone's forehead creased in a frown.

"I don't believe I know him *or* his shop," he said. "Why d'you ask?"

"Because he was the most uncivil wretch I've ever run into, but he sold me this book for a fraction of its real worth. I was ready to throttle him half a dozen times in the quarter hour I spent there."

"Throttle him," laughed Johnstone. "You? I can't believe that, old boy. You put on a grim front for the world at large, and tear hell out of it on a regular basis with those articles, but most of us know you a bit better than that..."

"Well it's true just the same. He left off slanging me after a while, but just as I was beginning to think he wasn't such a bad old creature after all, he started in on me again and I stormed out of the place."

"I'll do some checking for you, if you like," offered Johnstone. "Did you get a card from him?"

Thomas rummaged in the pockets of his greatcoat. "I did have one," he said, "but I must have left it behind."

"No matter then. Chilton...in Bedford Street."

Thomas nodded.

"That should be enough," said his friend. "I'll ask around and get back t'you in a week or so...meanwhile, I think I'll shove off before the snow buries us here. That storm outside promises t'be a big one."

He tossed off his glass and began the reverse ritual of bundling himself back into his outer clothing.

"Well I'm off, Tommy old boy," he said at length, tucking the tails of his scarf into his coat. "Keep at that book of yours..."

Thomas waved him a distracted farewell and nursed his brace of toddies well into the dinner hour.

By the time he left the Dragon's Jaws the city was close to knee-deep in snow, the skies an unbroken shroud of grey-white that seemed to sink closer and closer to the earth with each passing hour, dissolving rooftops and devouring streetlamps in its thick haze. As he trudged down the West Abbey Road and turned finally into Boar's Head Lane, he stopped for a moment to shake a clot of wet snow from his left shoulder and, in the breathy whisper of the storm, realised he was entirely alone.

"I don't know when the Road was ever as quiet as it is now," he murmured aloud, looking back the way he had come. The City had been transformed into a place of featureless shadows, broken at whiles by the gleam of light from a second- or third-storey window, the lambent aura of a streetlamp. "I wonder....what would it be like... to live in a world that was always like this...?"

The thought intrigued him, continued to grow in his mind until his speculations became boundless, and he found that with very little effort he could imagine himself in a place he might once have been before, a place of almost ceaseless snows, where the horizon of even the most far-seeing creatures was never an inch farther than a few hundred paces in any direction. It was almost like a memory of something he once might have experienced...

"Incredible..." he whispered into the snow haze, and turned for the last leg of his trek homeward, making sure his parcel was snugly safe inside his coat. When he looked up he found a tall figure barring his way—a woman, swathed in white furs, snow-white hair wafting in the wind, and a pale face of shadows from which gleamed two pale eyes the colour of winter ice in sunset.

"Come with me...please..."she said, and her voice was an echo of bells that thrilled him. "Come with me..."

She seemed to float away into the night, merge with the beckoning light of a corner streetlamp. Thomas reached out a hand to stay her, but she was gone even as he stumbled after her. He knew a brief moment of vaguely-remembered terror, but then:

"Wait!" he cried. "Where are you? How can I follow if...?"

A window overhead and across the lane came up and an angry voice threatened him with violence if he would not let honest folks sleep peaceful in their beds. Thomas growled a surly reply and, in a confusion of anger and utter bewilderment, stalked to his door, inserted his latchkey and stamped up the two flights to his rooms.

Once inside, he flung his scarf and greatcoat into a corner, kicked off his boots and faced the clutter of books, papers and what-not else that filled the apartment—tumbling across the floors and climbing the very walls to his waist in some places, and all in all covering most of the worn and threadbare wreckage that passed for his furnishings.

"The devil!" he snarled. "Have I gone full circle and come back to that wretched shop? And I know there's a carpet on the floor somewhere, but I'll be thrashed if I know where to look for it first...or if I dare look for it at all. Who knows what may have taken root down there under all this mess?"

He stood in the middle of his sitting-cum-workroom with a sudden and very deep discontent rising up inside him as he surveyed what was, at best, the very sordid thing he called home.

"Damn it, Beverley! It's no wonder you can't get any work done in this place. It's wringing you dry with chaos. Where...how...are you going to find any kind of inspiration in a place like this? Monday would have died here..."

A slow fury began to mount in him, an urge to toss everything into the nearest dustbin and draw the cover down over all of it, himself and his might-as-well-be-non-existent novel included as well...and then he looked down at the brown-papered parcel clutched in the fist he'd been brandishing at the walls and his anger slipped away in a foolish smile.

"But not tonight," he said softly. "Tonight's for a pot of tea and *Silver Stars*..."

A few minutes later, with an armchair unearthed, a lamp beside him and a mug of evil-smelling Souchong in his lap, Thomas turned to the first page of his dearly-bought treasure...

When he awoke, it was morning outside his windows and the rear board of Monday's book—covered in cornflower blue cloth with a floral-leaf design stamped in silver—winked up at him from his lap. The storm seemingly had continued on through the night, heavy clots of snow still clinging to the glass panes and sill. Thomas stretched lazily, set his book carefully aside and waded through the sea of papers on the floor to look down on a thoroughly unfamiliar Boar's Head Lane—an ocean of snow that swept, unbroken as far as he could see in either direction—and, directly beneath his window, a fur-swathed figure who smiled up at him through the watery half-light of morning.

"Come with me..." she said to him, and the fact that he could hear her voice ever so softly but quite clearly through the glass did not trouble him in the least.

"What do you want with me?" he asked in a hoarse whisper, and again, "What do you want with me?"

"You must come with me," she replied. "IYou will remember someday...but now you must come.... please..."

A gust of wind sent a diaphanous curtain of snow swirling down from the rooftops and when he looked again she was gone. Thomas stared at where she had been, and then thought to see her at the corner where Boar's Head met with the Abbey Road. Her bell-like voice seemed to float on the wind, a lingering music that whispered to him again and again:

"You must come with me...please...come... with...me..."

He never stopped to consider what madness drove him out into the streets of the City that day, only that *she* had begged him to follow her and suddenly he wanted nothing more than just that—to follow her out into the white wastes, to the very ends of the earth if that was where she would lead him. Clothed again in his greatcoat, gloves and scarf, armed against the chill by a flask of wretched brandy in one pocket, he set out into the *terra incognita* of the City and virtually swam through the storm in her wake.

Each time he thought he had lost her a trill of delighted laughter would waft through the haze to show him the way, or he would catch a glimpse of her on the next street corner... and the sun, hidden though it was by the lowering clouds, rose up one side of the sky and began its downward way upon the other...until Thomas, in mid-afternoon, found himself among the dark facades and stonework of the warehouses that lined the harbour, and realised he had been led back again to Bedford Street, and the tatty old shop of Edmund Chilton was no more than half a block away.

"Why on earth would I come back here?" Thomas puzzled, but his feet already were moving down the steps to the door of the shop, now swept free of snow. He stepped through the clangour of the bell, saw Chilton seated behind his desk with a book on his lap and a massive marmalade tabby perched on the desk beside him.

"Well look what one of your brothers dragged in, Samantha," boomed the bookseller. "Didn't think I'd lay eyes on you again, Beverley. I see you've been through the book. What'd you think of it?"

"It was the best of them all," said Thomas. "I was there, standing beside the Princess Eos in the northern waste kingdoms as we fought to save her land from the Ice Giants."

"Great stuff, eh?"

"It was magic."

Chilton nodded. "Magic indeed. But why are you back here? You're not going t'make a habit out of this are you? Samantha hates interruptions when we're reading."

"She's beautiful," murmured Thomas, reaching out a tentative hand. When the cat darted a raspy pink tongue at his fingers and began to purr, he beamed, scratching gently at the great ruff of fur around her neck. "She just sits and keeps you company while you read?"

Chilton looked puzzled.

"No...she sits here and listens while I read to her," he said.

"She *listens* while you read," said Thomas.

"Well of course she listens while I read," huffed Chilton. "What else would you expect her t'do? Besides...she hates missing anything...especially the illustrations."

Thomas did not even try to hide his skepticism.

"D'you mean t'tell me that—?"

"Every word, young feller," nodded the bookseller. "She's the toughest literary critic I know...or she would be, if she felt like writing things down. I know when we've got ourselves a winner when she brings family to listen as well...especially that big grey lives on the other side of town. I'll likely be reading this again to a full house tomorrow."

He offered up the dust-wrapped volume to where Thomas could read the title.

"*Mina and the Magic Mooncat*," he said aloud. "By Randolph Jordan Sutherland. I've never heard of him."

"Well now you have," replied Chilton, and if you like Lanky Jeff Monday you'll like Randy Jay Sutherland as well." In answer to Beverley's unspoken question he said, "We had word-game plays on each other's names."

"Really? What'd they call you?"

Chilton grinned an evil grin. "Cranky," he said with vast pleasure.

Beverley cocked his head to one side. "Wait a minute! Monday wrote his books over a hundred years ago."

"What's your point?" said Chilton.

For some reason he could not explain, Thomas realised he had no point, or if he had had one it was gone. Chilton seemed unfazed.

"Anyway, *Mooncat* is a pretty good piece of work in spite of being much younger than Mondays's stuff. Tad on the light side, but some o' the best stuff ever written has been that way. Samantha thinks it's the whiskers, and not just because of the title."

Thomas drew his hand back from the cat's chin as if he'd been stung, his eyes going saucer-size with surprise.

"She...she just nodded!" he exclaimed, staring at her.

"She doesn't believe in over-reacting, unlike at least one of us in the room," said Chilton casually. "You must know how cats are about their dignity...but tell me more of your thoughts on *Silver Stars*..."

Beverley shook his head. "It was just wonderful," he said. "I can't say more than that because it was—"

"Yes...magic, as you said," agreed Chilton softly. "Jeff certainly did know his business. He lounged back in his chair, musing aloud, "Who can forget Rinaldo's harrowing journey to Land's Edge, to save the stars from annihilation at the hands of the wicked archimage Darkbundle... led ever onward through all the deception by the enchanted crystal given him by the princess Eos herself...or when the Ice Giants besieged the Snow Palace, how Rinaldo's beloved Desdemona gave her life to help save the kingdom. Chilton shook his head in admiration. "Not many people could have written that last scene..."

His trancy mutterings were interrupted by the sound of the bell above the door as a tallish, bespectacled gentleman in a grey overcoat entered the shop. Chilton leaned across his desk, giving Samantha a little boost in the direction of the back room.

"Thomas," he said," consulting a gold watch extracted from a pocket in his dressing gown, "why don't you come back at closing time," he said gently. "This fellow's an old friend I've not seen in a dog's age...sorry, Samantha...but if you could come back in an hour or so, I'll conjure us up something for supper and we can talk some more. Whattayasay?"

Beverley nodded dreamily. "Sounds fair t'me. So I'll be back before you close up then," he said.

He turned, muttered a polite greeting to the older gentleman in response to the latter's smile, and walked towards the door of the shop with a puzzled expression on his face. Then he shook himself once, and went out into the street. Chilton rose to greet the newcomer.

"Kip," he said warmly. "So good t'see you again.

"Good t'see you as well, Cranky. Been all over hell's half-acre trying to find you this time. I see you're still up to your old tricks."

Chilton grinned. "You mean Beverley," he said, nodding towards the door. "True enough. He's got some promise though, just needs the right kind of inspiration. By the way, Samantha and I went through *The Man Who Would Be King* just last week...for the umpteenth time. Still your best..."

Thomas came through the door of the shop just as Chilton, who had exchanged his Oriental dressing gown for a maroon velvet smoking jacket and a knotted grey silk ascot, was dousing the lights in the window. He reached under his greatcoat and brought out two paper bags.

"The wine's for our dinner," he said quickly. "The other is for Samantha. I managed to find a grocer who was willing to braise some beef for her. I hope she likes that sort of thing..."

Chilton made a great show of adjusting his monocle.

"You bet she does...but come this way, my boy," he said, leading Beverley towards the rear of the shop. "There's more to Edmund Chilton's Second Hand and Rare Everything Emporium than meets the eye. And before I forget..."

He made a quick detour back to his desk and came up with another brown-papered parcel that he handed to Thomas.

"From Samantha," he explained. "It's an extra copy of *Mooncat*. She was quite certain it belonged in your collection. You can leave your coat and things here."

Thomas divested himself of outerwear and accepted the book wordlessly, followed the bookseller into the back room and thence up a short flight of stairs where a furred silhouette at its head purred with pleasure as he neared the top.

"Thank you, Samantha..." was all he could manage before the softly-lit room that swam into view struck him speechless.

It was like an opulent version of the shop downstairs without the clutter and chaos—warm and close with thick wine-red carpets, the polished sheen of old wood, velvets and brocades, glass-fronted cabinets and bric-a-brac shelves overflowing with feathers, antique glass, books and tiny figurines in bronze and brass that gleamed and glinted in the candlelight from a small table set with silver and spotless white linen. Thomas stood in the doorway, oblivious to the cat curling about his ankles and her vocal demands for a scratch behind the ears.

My God," he whispered, awe-struck and then some. "I've never seen...it's so...and these tiny sculptures...with every detail perfect. I've got a friend who would kill..."

He picked up a two-inch high figure from a shelf by the door—a small mouse in a bandleader's costume, complete with paper-thin whispers—and looked at Chilton with rapturous eyes.

"They're marvellous," he said. "Where did you get them? There's bloody hundreds of them!"

"You like 'em, eh?"

"Like them? No I love them they're incredible."

Chilton handed him a small cardboard box.

"Good. Here's a dozen of my best."

Thomas went speechless a second time as the bookseller grinned and Samantha purred

and then Chilton served supper whilst she purred some more and Thomas said a great many things he never remembered having said to anyone...and the next thing he knew dinner was over and they were sunk in fathoms of armchair, with coffee and brandy and Chilton firing up another of his stinky old briers.

"So whattaya do t'keep the wolves away, Thomas?" came the bookseller's voice from behind a cloud of smoke. Beverley hung his head ruefully.

"Not very much, I'm afraid," he said quietly. "I'm what most people would call an *aspiring* writer."

"*Per*spiring on the days when you buy books a bit much for your means."

"That too," agreed Thomas.

"What sort of stuff d'you write?"

Thomas examined the light in his brandy.

"The usual things, I suppose," he said almost bitterly. "Articles, stories, anything that'll bring in a bit of cash while I'm about trying to write something worthwhile..."

He looked up with a strange bewildered look on his face.

"But I'll tell you something Mister Chilton—"

"Edmund, please..."

"Edmund. In the last little while I've been thinking quite a bit about what I've been doing and...well...I muck about with a perfectly marvellous bunch of people, dear superlatively creative friends, steadfast and true...yet I spend most of *my* time writing about everything that's wrong with our lives, dragging my characters through the worst things imaginable, slanging the dickens out of people who can't appreciate the brightness around them, and generally sounding off like a damn fool because deep down I'm really just like them..."

"And now you've had a change of heart?" inquired Chilton quietly, arching one of his feathery eyebrows.

"You're damned right I have!" Thomas said emphatically, with an image of a strange woman in white furs flitting through a snowscape in his mind. "Just talking about it now made me realise that people like Monday had the right idea of it. I saw all the silver stars and I heard Eos singing...and then after I'd helped to save the world and Darkbundle was dogmeat...she kissed me...said I was a hero...

"I mean, it's not like my life is one wretched day after another, yet if I ever finish the novel I've supposedly been writing for the last year, someone reading it will think... well...I don't know what they'll think and suddenly I don't want t'know..."

He stared down into his brandy again.

"I suppose what I'm trying to say is you can never have enough magic in the world, and I should be trying to add to it, instead of tearing it all down."

A faint smile lifted the corners of Edmund Chilton's mouth.

"You could do a lot worse, Thomas," he murmured, raising his glass in a salutation. "You could do a lot worse..."

Chilton watched him walk off into the night, and smiled as he relocked the door of the shop. He wandered through the ranks of bookcases for a while; in darkness he reached out to touch the bindings of favoured volumes, as he would have reached out to greet old friends, warming himself with the memories of each one. Then he knocked over the pile of magazines on principle and when he went back to his desk for one last pipe before going to bed, he found Samantha on the blotter, keeping a close eye on her favourite book, and the tattered remnants of a small white business card.

"Well, old girl," he said softly, a counterpoint to her rumblings of contentment. "What say we add this one to the scrapbook."

He picked up the business card Beverley had left behind the day before and put it in the pocket of his smoking jacket, shuffled the cheque he had torn up earlier into a waste basket.

"D'you remember that shop we had in London back in '93, Samantha...or that hole-in-the-wall in Paris where we sold copies of *Les Trois Mousquetaires* with the ink barely dry on the pages?

"Some things don't change, me proud beauty, so long as there are people making magic in the world...and it was good t'see old Kip again..."

He put another match to his pipe and briefly considered a second stroll about the shop.

"Ah...come on, Samantha, let's pack up and be on our way. I'm a bit hurt the kid didn't recognize me as the model for Rinaldo, but I suppose he had more important things on his mind."

He reached into a drawer of the desk and drew out a slim volume that he regarded in the soft glow of embers from his pipe, laughing quietly to himself.

"I wonder who we'll be next time around, Sam," he whispered. "I wonder what Beverley would have said if I'd shown him this."

And in the small pool of light, he smiled down at a copy of *The Snow King's Daughter*... by Thomas Beverley.

Hundreds of leagues to the east, in the long shadows cast by mountains over a land that had disappeared into the realms of myth and legendry, a living creature guised as a woman stood by the door of a dilapidated wooden hut and gazed with pale sightless eyes into the night. It was bitterly cold, the wind howled and whipped the long silver length of her hair into tangles around a body scarcely concealed by the ragged clothing pressed against it.

She was older than the world itself, spawned in the dawn of Time that in time, brought mankind to her doorstep in the middle of a barren waste...to build a town they named, all unknowing...with her name...*Skaistykla*... and created a small hell on earth to serve the warlords and the priests and the demons that lived in their daily lives and in their worst nightmares.

She lifted her head into the wind, sniffed at whatever it was her distorted senses could cull from what went racing by on the claws of the storm. If she was deemed blind by those who came to her, what she saw with her inner sight was far more discerning.

She knew she had only done what she felt was necessary to survive; that in serving those who came to her, who fed her life-force, she had become a whore to all that was base and contemptible in the human animal. No one ever came to her for goodness. They came to fuck her. They came to ask for revenge...payback for the smallest most petty grievances imaginable...and she spread her legs to all of them...took small bloody chunks of their souls...or their coins, if there was nothing of value to be found within the envelopes of flesh that gave them a semblance of life.

She stood awhiles in the storm, suddenly cold and shivering, sent a silent prayer of the deepest gratitude up into the night, to the unseen stars and the endless turning of worlds alive and dead around them. In her mind's eye she found the recent memory of a young man who had come to her—as they all had come—to ask for blood...to whom she had *given* blood...but sent on his way having extracted a promise to remember her...

Tonight she felt the fulfillment of his promise, and wept for the first time in all the centuries of her existence. She turned, went back inside, lay down on rags and the ancient ravaged pelt of a mountain wolf, and closed her sightless eyes to the world, saw instead the reality of her being.

Above her she raised up a shiny silken thread that moved in the air above her like a snake writhing in the throes of Death.

THE UNFADNG FLOWER

She stretched it out above her, gentled it into a peaceful shimmer of light...sighed...drew it taut between her hands and snapped it in two...

"Now I can go free," she said...

Back Pages

It was well into the spring before the small storm surrounding the "mysterious disappearance" of the artist Aengus Robertson died down. The authorities spent weeks and then months chasing after every whisper of what were no clues at all, and finally left off chasing anything, professing themselves to be totally in the dark, and closed the case with the equivalent of a shrug of their bureaucratic shoulders. The inspector in charge of the investigation was heard to remark that she had never encountered such a case before, and fervently hoped never to encounter one like it ever again. By mid-May even the City newspapers had lost interest, and thereafter it was left only to those two who knew something of the answer to the riddle to carry on.

Nicholas and Brandywine said nothing. The events of that night became a secret shared by them alone, the source of occasional glances that passed between them when no one else was paying attention, brief words of speculation and puzzlement when they were alone. Nicholas had taken a match to Robertson's few words of farewell; Brandy had neatly folded away the small pile of clothing they had found on the floor. Before first light of the next day, it was only a small clutch of the local cat population who witnessed the pair of them spirit a shrouded canvas across the courtyard of St John's Mews and down into the cellar of Windy's house. In the very midst of the initial uproar, a barrister who had acted as Robertson's agent made it known to the police that the previous summer, the artist had made it plain to him that a young man named Nicholas Wyndham was to be the executor and the sole beneficiary of his estate:

"...He said there was no one else...Wyndham had become a close friend...he could do with Robertson's belongings and assets as he chose...he was confident Wyndham would know what to do with all of it..."

So for a time, Windy became the prime suspect in the mystery—the only suspect, in actual fact—until it became obvious to all concerned that he had absolutely no reason to do away with the missing artist, and had in truth been on the best of terms with him for the entire length of their association.

The apple trees had blossomed all round the courtyard. The cats once again had taken up a perpetual daytime occupation of the branches. Hearthstones were swept clean of ashes, windows secured against lingering night-time chills now were thrown open, draperies drawn back to allow the light and perfume of a new springtide to drive out the staleness of winter. In the upstairs music room of Wyndham's house, Brandy sipped a mug of coffee and gazed out across the courtyard.

"It will be so strange," she said softly. "He would have been the first one out there... pretending to growl at the cats...pretending to be all huffy with the rest of the world. He always seemed happy to see me...but sad at the same time."

That complete truth of that was Windy's secret, something he felt Robertson would not have wanted to be shared with anyone.

"I think you reminded him of someone he once knew..."

"I was so afraid I'd been too forward with him, Windy. Now I'm just gonna miss him..."

"Me too."

They drank coffee for a little while, standing beside each other at the windows, watching the courtyard come alive, the sun sneaking over top of the surrounding towers, glancing off the gilded cross atop the church at the entrance to the Mews.

"What are you going t'do with all his things? Have you decided? And what about the...painting...downstairs. It scares me a little, I don't know why..."

"Maybe we should leave that where it is for now," he said. "As for the rest, I've been thinking about it the last few days. I know he'd be pleased if we set aside some of his money for the care and feeding of those little furry goblins in the trees...and then some for the shelters, for four-foots *and* two-foots..."

She nodded, knowing that he was thinking of her. "That sounds wonderful. He was right to let you be the one to decide."

Nicholas had never been so certain of that, but of a sudden there was something definite in his mind.

"Branny, I'm going to go away for a few days," he said. "You're welcome to stay here while I'm gone, of course. And now that he's finally found some new digs I'm sure Andy would appreciate a bit of help moving his things..."

The next day he packed a travel-bag for a week or so, hired a motor-car and followed his nose northward. By lunchtime he had left the City behind him, the ribbon of paved road beneath him winding alongside the river as the city streets became riparian marshland to his left and the rolling hills of farmland to his right. The tufts of wintered cat-tails had already begun to go from wheat colour to green again, the farmland fields showed neatly- spaced furrows and the first tiny spears of corn sprouting upward into the light. Windy felt utterly at peace for the first time in months.

With the coming of night he was halfway to the Carillon, now heading directly northward rather than following the river. He found a room and his supper at a small inn just off the road, in the middle of endless-seeming pastureland, fell dreamlessly into sleep to the sound of milk cows coming home for the night. In the morning, before setting out again, he drank black coffee fragrant with chicory, and breakfasted on warm new cheese and biscuits still hot from the oven of his hosts. By mid-afternoon he had turned off the paved roads, heading northeastward on narrow lanes rutted with the wheels of farm wagons, and quite suddenly finding himself leaning forward over the wheel of his car with something that could be nothing else but excitement...anticipation...

It had been more than three years since he had been home.

And then it was there before him, high up on the hillside, the single-storeyed sprawl of the place where he had been born and grown into young adulthood, every turn and twist of the drive upward familiar, every ancient oak that rose up beside it an old friend. He came to the paved court enclosed by the half-circle of the house itself, switched off the engine of his car, and saw the faces of servants in the windows lighting up with recognition, and his mother at the door...curious...and then he could hear her cry of surprise and delight as she rushed forward to embrace him.

"Nicky," she whispered, with her arms around him and her lips like the soft sting of love-struck bees on his cheeks. "My baby...oh...Nicky you've come home..."

She was scarcely changed at all from how he remembered her—still straight and slender and elegant as any farm-wife, her beautiful stormcloud eyes clear and bright, her hair a crown of silver-blond with only the first touch of grey as it settled down again on her shoulders.

He said, "Mum," and they wept for joy of each other.

"...You never said you were coming."

"I didn't know until just the night before yesterday."

"You'll stay now?"

"No, Mum, I can't just yet. I've got some business up north, but I'll spend some time on my way back, I promise."

"I've missed you so much. I know you've written, but it's not the same. Are you all right? Are you happy where you are? I worry so much for you, Nicky. I shouldn't have let your brothers treat you so poorly."

He shrugged.

"Mum, I don't blame them so much. I'm not ungrateful for all the things I have in this world, but having the last word on all of it was never what I wanted, even if Chaunce, Raymond and William never understood that. T'them I was just one more player in the game to win the Wyndham legacy from Father.

"Where I am now...making music in the big city...I have no struggles, no dire threats to my existence...and as much as I appreciate what you and Father send my way each month, if all I had was the friends I've found there, I'd still be wealthy beyond measure."

He went to his travel-bag and brought out the exquisitely-embroidered shawl he'd bought for her, and a packet of drawings and photographs to show her something of his life away from home. One by one he named each of his friends to her, told her something of each of them...why they were, to him, the best family he could ever have hoped for.

"...We're all just a bit different from everyone and everything around us, so we get along...watch out for each other. Someday you and Da can visit and you'll see...I'm all right, Mum. You don't have t'worry about me..."

A few hours later they sat in the kitchen with their supper, on wooden stools worn smooth by the bum-sides of the servants, the sunset behind them turning the world outside the east-facing windows into copper and crimson.

"I hate having meals all alone in the dining room when everyone's gone," she said. "Your father and the boys are all off to Amworth over something or another. It's so wonderful to have you here, all to myself."

They left off paying any attention to their dinner plates; when Alexandra Wyndham leaned towards him Nicholas put an arm round her shoulders and they sat that way in silence. What she might have thought or felt could be surmised, but he put his face down into her hair and inhaled, became dizzy in the flood of his childhood coming back to him, the days when his brothers teased him without mercy for being so different from any one of them, for seeking his mother's company when they were out raising hell in the countryside, or plotting ways to outdo each other in their father's eyes.

"You don't have to be so cautious with your heart, Nicky," she said. "A little bit of hurt or disappointment is nothing, and it's always worth it in the end, no matter how dreadful it feels then. Any one of your friends... they're all so beautiful..."

"It's not like that, Mum. I look after them. I'm older."

"You're just afraid to care too much," she said quietly.

After supper they went outdoors, down through his mother's garden, where prized roses only just beginning to flower in the new season vied for attention with the first promise of tomatoes and cucumbers and whatnot else that would feed them and a great many others through the summer. At length they turned away from the house, started down the far hillside to the stables, and he could hear the whicker of a voice he knew very well.

"He knows you're here," she said.

Amadeus stood in the growing shadows of the stable, a massive creature Nicholas had looked after when it was only just learning to stand on four wobbly legs, now grown into an almost monstrous jet-black draft horse, seventeen hands high, midnight feathers adorning each hoof the size of one of the plates they'd left behind in the kitchen. His snort and snuffle of welcome cut through the hum of cicadas outside, flanks thundering against the rails of his stall as he turned to greet his own childhood companion. The great head came down upon

Windy's shoulder, stayed there as he stroked his neck, ran his fingers through the mane that reached almost to the ground.

"I was hoping I could take him north with me, instead of the car," he said.

His mother smiled. "I'll make sure Tam has him ready for you in the morning..."

That night in the great room, Nicholas sat down to the piano and played to the audience he had known as a child—his mother, the housemaids Tasha and Celine, gameskeeper Finn, Tam from the stables, and Aaron, who managed all the grounds of the Wyndham holdings. In this place that had been home, his had not been the only music, but now at whiles he thought he could hear a different voice, similar to the one he'd discovered in the City, but this one belonging to the earth itself, indifferent to the strivings of those who spent a moment of Infinity there, and then were gone.

When the piano fell silent, they bid him goodnight one by one, remembering him as "the young master" who had never had a harsh word for any of them, who all too often went along with them at their chores, rather than sit idly by while they worked in his service.

He went upstairs to his old bedroom...drowsed in the sweet nighttime scent of his past... smiled sleepily as his mother tucked a blanket closer round his chin, leaned over to kiss him goodnight.

"You don't have to be so cautious with your heart, Nicky," she said again. "Don't be afraid..."

He and the mountain masquerading as a horse were gone at first light, down the hillside and back onto the high road winding north into the dales and valleys north of the Carillon.

Amadeus refused to amble, broke into thundering gallops and playful caracoles, nipping at the toes of Windy's boots, tossing his head into the rarefied air of reunion with his beloved boy.

It was another day of traveling, though now without the hum of the motor car's engine, or the smell of oil and petrol to desecrate the sweet smell of the land before *progress* came along. They passed through ancient woods and crossed rivulets that knew voice long before ever the hand or speech of Man was known. At one point, suddenly dizzy with the scent of newly-bloomed lilac, he and Amadeus had to cut a wide arc through a neighbouring field to avoid the cloud of honey-bees buzzing in and around the stand. Near the end of their journey, Nicholas again found the Findhorn rushing southward, growing wider and deeper with every small stream that leapt down from the hillsides to add snow-melt and dewfall to its flood. Glen Carrick came at nightfall, and the familiar welcoming shadow of the public house where he had come with his father and siblings a decade before. The proprietor looked at him curiously until recognition came to him, and Nicholas grinned in return.

"It's been a while," he said, and the innkeeper nodded as he took down Windy's name, accepted payment for his stay. "I don't care what you do with me, but don't stint a moment *or* expense when it comes to Amadeus outside. He's a prince among his kind and I'll not have him treated otherwise."

That being said, Windy's things were taken upstairs whilst he and his host repaired to the taproom for something to wash away the dust of travel as an evening meal was prepared.

"I'm looking for an old family," said Windy as he leaned against the bar, took a long draught from the tankard of ale splashed down in front of him. "The Robertsons, if you can tell me where t'find them…"

The innkeeper, whose name as Windy remembered it was Rickard Danforth, shook his head.

"I don't know of any Robertsons hereabouts," he said, but squinted as he gave it a second thought in deference to Windy as a respected bit of custom.

Nicholas pondered that a moment, dismayed he had come so far on what suddenly seemed to be a fool's errand.

"Are you sure?" he asked. "A family of one son and six daughters, their father being the blacksmith…?"

Rickard Danforth cocked his head to one side and then begged a moment while he sent his own son off. Half an hour and another tankard of ale later, the young one returned from a visit to his grandfather.

"… My father says you're looking for the Ardreys," he said. "Years ago they lived here in the village, but the boy ran afoul of old Dorion de Montenay…fell in love with his eldest daughter, and then, for pride and spite, de Montenay hounded them to their deaths in the falls above the river…"

In morning sunshine Nicholas walked down the high street of Glen Carrick, turned right and then left towards the outskirts of the village and then followed the burble of a stream until he came to a large two-storeyed, half-timbered house and the falling-down remains of a deserted smithy. He let himself in through a gate in the rail fence surrounding the front yard, picked his way across it on a flagstone path that already seemed in danger of being overrun by thistle and creeper vines from the small garden beside it. He knocked on the heavy iron-hinged door and waited...finally heard light footsteps drawing closer...

"Good morning," he said to the woman who opened it, "I hope I'm not too early."

She was of medium height, in her early fifties. Sturdy best described her, with long salt-and-pepper hair once a deep brown, and dark eyes that looked him a cautious welcome. She wiped her hands on the homespun apron she wore over a light cotton dress patterned with cornflowers.

"Not at all," she said. "I'm up with the sun...and this one..."

She nodded down to her bare feet where a small curly-haired terrier stood silently, no doubt ready and waiting should there be need to attack Windy's boots.

"I'm looking for Camille Ardrey?" he said.

"Cami," she replied with a half smile. "Only my parents ever called me Camille."

She studied his face for a moment or two, then stood aside, inviting him into the shaded interior of the house, led him down a central hall into a broad kitchen glowing in the morning light. There she turned, offering him a seat at a long wooden table, and a mug of steaming coffee from a metal pot on the wood-stove.

"Black is fine," he said.

"You're Alex Wyndham's youngest, aren't you?" she asked. To Windy's look of surprise, she went, "Nicholas. I know you *and* your mum from the fall harvest markets in Aylesbury. You look just like her, one of the prettiest ladies I've ever known, and every bit as generous with her good fortune."

Nicholas ducked his head over his coffee, embarrassed for himself, but secretly pleased that someone should speak so well of his mother. The little brindled terrier bustled his way to a blanket set beside the wood-stove, fussed for moment before settling down with his chin on his front paws, watching them with curious black-button eyes. Nicholas didn't know where to begin and an awkward silence fell over them, until Camille Ardrey... Cami to all but her parents...sat across from him with her own mug.

"She's missed you," she said. "You went down t'the City a while back."

He nodded.

"And now you're home for good?"

This time he shook his head.

"No, ma'am," he said. "I know I should've visited long ago...but for now I've come in service to a friend. A man named Aengus Robertson, who said he came from this village, the son of the local smith, the only son of seven children."

He watched her eyes widen at his last words, then grow heart-breakingly sad.

"We had a brother once," she whispered. "Alain...he fell in love with the local lord's daughter and she with him. They died together in the falls just the east of the village when I was very young. It seems t'have become a bit of a tradition in our family, dying before our time. There's only three of us left now."

Windy's mind raced, pulling bits and snippets of knowledge together.

"I think the young man who was your brother did die that night, ma'am," he said slowly, "but it was different from the kind of Death we're used to...the way things end for most of us. Aengus Robertson said that he watched the river carry Rochelle de Montenay away from him and it was more than he could bear."

Her eyes went far away, looking backward into the past.

"I was his favourite, and it was like being a princess when he would bring me little gifts, or go out of his way to play with me. He was so handsome and I was so jealous of all the girls who just threw themselves at his feet. I wasn't even five years old, but I knew I would never know anyone like him in all my life...

"In my heart I've known all along he didn't die that night. I always wondered why he never came home...never once wrote to tell me where he was."

They drank their coffee, darting looks at each other the while, Nicholas desperately seeking for some way to do what he felt should be done without worsening the deep sorrow come to her eyes.

"Your brother was badly injured in the fall," he said, "spent days in the water, carried along until some river-folk pulled him out and saw to his hurts. When he was recovered enough to travel again, he just went in the direction he had been going and came to the City...became Aengus Robertson...became an artist whose paintings became very well known there and abroad. We became neighbours three years ago, but it took those three years and a strange series of occurrences for him to tell me his story...and I don't think he ever considered that I would come here..."

"Why *did* you come, Nicholas?" she asked.

"He was quite well off...Cami...and he named me as the executor of his estate."

"So now he's truly gone," she said, turning away from him, her voice become hoarse and broken.

"Yes...I think so...or whatever it is that rules our lives has made off with him again, as it seemed to you years ago. In any case, while I intended to give most everything away where it could be of some good for those who were in need, it occurred to me that his family, if there were any yet living, should have the better part of it, and they should be the ones to decide, not me."

She turned back to him, suddenly so much like her brother, if only that she felt no shame in her tears, that there was no reason to hide honest grief.

"There are lots of nieces and nephews," she said. "They'll wonder to learn that the uncle they never knew was a famous artist...and as for myself and my sisters and their husbands, we've no one of us ever had much more than enough to get by, even when Father was alive and still working the forge...so...

"Thank you, Nicholas, for the news and for your own generosity, and the trouble you've gone to. I won't pretend that Alain's money will be unappreciated; I hope he found some peace from losing Rochelle like that. I only met her once or twice...and I was very small...but she was lovely and very sweet to me. I wasn't jealous of her...not at all..."

"Did you not have a family of your own then?"

"I was in love with my brother, Alain Ardrey," she said. "I suppose losing him was like him losing Rochelle..."

They talked through the morning, Camille telling him stories of her childhood and the person whom he had known as Aengus Robertson. They made arrangements for her to become the arbiter of her brother's possessions, and she made lunch for them, out on the back porch that overlooked the mill-race that had served the forge, and on to the next rise of hills growing green in the coming-of-summer sunshine. As they finished their meal, and he turned to go, they embraced and she thanked him again, offered him a place to stay should he ever come that way again. At the door, Windy had one last question.

"Cami...you said you knew in your heart that Alain was still alive."

"I did. I knew it."

"You were that close," he said.

She nodded slowly. "Travel safely, Nicholas, and give my love to your mother. Tell her I'll see her again at Aylesbury market come fall harvest..."

"I will," he said; and then, "I know he never forgot you, Cami. I know you were ever in his thoughts and in his heart..."

He went back to the inn, then spent the remainder of his day wandering the countryside, relieved to have kept faith with Alain Ardrey's trust in him. As the afternoon wore on he found himself walking the banks of the river, and then to the cliffs over the falls, where he stood in the sunset and listened to the rush and roar of the water as it plunged to the plains below. He became lost in it, oblivious to everything around him, until a gentle touch on his arm startled him back into awareness...

The following day he began a leisurely trip back to the Carillon, this time following the course of the river wherever possible, finding solace in the companionship of Amadeus and the newfound sense of peace in his heart. Once again his mother greeted him, went arm-in-arm with him, following Amadeus as Tam led him back to the stables and a well-earned reward of sweet alfalfa grass and a bucket of new carrots.

The next day in late afternoon as he sat in the shade of the house, softly playing on the small violin he had learned with as a child, he saw a familiar figure on horseback cantering up the drive. He stood to greet his father, felt his mother's presence behind him, come to do the same.

Frederick Wyndham came to within a few paces of his son, stood silently for a handful of heartbeats before striding forward to embrace him.

"You mother sent for me," he said. "I didn't say anything to your brothers, left them t'look after things in Amworth. I thought it might be a good thing for us t'be able to talk and such, without them acting like a bunch of hungry savages. You can stay for a while...?"

Windy nodded. "Yes, sir," he said "A few days, at any rate...", and was rewarded by a smile from his mother.

After dinner at the long table in the dining room, Alexandra left her husband and youngest son with a new bottle of brandy, and an inner prayer of gratitude to see them come together after such a long time.

"Yer mum says you're doin' well, that you've got friends to depend on, and a growing reputation for your music."

Windy nodded.

"I never wanted t'see you go."

"I know that, Da. It means everything that you let me, and in such wise that I'm free to become... whatever..."

"Will you play for me before you go?"

"Of course I will."

"And your business, that brought you here and up the dales, it went well...?"

"I think so. I can go back now with the knowing that I've done right by the person who trusted me t'do so."

The elder Wyndham leaned back in his chair and sipped brandy. The afterglow of the sunset cast its light through the tall windows beside them, cast shadows over his face.

"I want you t'know that I love you, Nicky," he said. "I know I let your brothers bully you, but I was wrong to let them do it. I wanted you to fight them for your place here, *show* them *you* were the one t'look after all of this after me. They're good lads but they're too much like me, too much concerned with the material things that have come to us, things that might never have come at all if Alexandra Bellefleur had not consented to marry me. And you're her son, Nicky, more like her than you are like me, and I value that more than anything else in the world except for her. I miss you here, but as long as I know you're happy where you are that's all right, I can live with it...easily...and make do with your brothers. Among the three of them maybe they'll be able do as well as you would have done on your own, but that's something will stay between just the two of us."

He grinned, reached out and took Windy's hand to seal the bargain of their secret.

"...Windy you're back!" cried Brandywine, and he allowed himself the luxury of one of her endless all-around hugs ending with the scent of her hair in his nostrils and a gentle kiss where the curve of his jaw met up with one ear.

"I am," he said. "What's with the cart out in the courtyard?"

"That's for the last of Andy's things," she said, not letting go. "He's moving into a flat in the old City...a wonderful little place on *Rue de l'espoir*...it's French and all full of poetry... and even better than all of that—"

Andrew appeared in that moment, on his way out the door with an armload of loose bits.

"Hello, Windy," he said.

"Hello yourself I guess I'm gonna miss you."

Brandy finally let go of Nicholas and said:

"Tell, Andy..."

"You tell, Brandy," said Andrew, colouring a deep flush of red.

"Are you sure?"

Andrew nodded.

"Andy's met someone!" she cried. "We went to a poetry reading two nights ago and there was this yummy boy there..."

"His name's Alain," Andrew said quickly. "He's been in the City for a while but he said he had lots of room and maybe I might like to move in...so right there we decided..."

Nicholas smiled, felt a bit of the world come round and right itself in the best fashion he could have imagined. He promised to visit the new digs in the next few days, pleading exhaustion from all the traveling he'd done, but knowing there was one thing he should do as soon as possible.

Later that night, when Brandy had come back bursting with curiosity, he related the entirety of his *adventure*, explaining all of it, and ending it with...

"...That same afternoon I went walking along the river, found myself on the cliffs above the falls, and that was where Robertson's sister found me again. She said there was one last thing she should tell me...

"...*You see, at the time I didn't know anything but that he was gone from my life, as any five-year old would be crushed by that kind of loss. Not long after, I tried to drown myself here, in the same place where I had lost him, and that's how I knew for certain he was still alive.*

"*My sisters saved me that day, but I was half-dead when they did, far enough along to wherever that I lost all sense of my grief or my terror or the world around me...only that I felt myself floating before this great ball of light that I knew was the End...and that Alain would have been there to guide me if he had gone before.*"

Three days later there was an article across the entire front page of the daily newspapers, all of them recounting an utterly strange occurrence in the harbour the night before. According to eyewitnesses Nicholas Wyndham, a local musician, and Brandywine Lloyd, a local artist, it was like nothing they'd ever seen before...

"...We were just out for a walk along the harbourfront when we noticed something floating out from where the Findhorn comes out to meet the sea...it looked like something about the height and width of a tall person, but very flat, floating on the surface of the water. What was so strange was that a tower of light seemed to pour upward from it, and when the light of the sunset met with it, there was this great explosion that sent the light streaming up into the sky...and then it was gone...just...gone..."

Dreams of Nubian Splendour

Windy and *les Boulevardiers* were holding court on the terrace of the Silver Rose. Spring had given way to the first days of summer but someone had forgotten to inform whoever was in charge that midsummer heat was inappropriate for early June. Nevertheless, though somewhat wilted in their ragtag finery, all were feeling flush with modest successes and doggedly pursued celebratory rounds of winter wine accompanied by a particularly tasty array of seafood snippets fresh off the fishing boats that morning.

Somewhere in the midst of their third-it-could-have-been-fourth round of frosty wine, Diana looked round their table with a frown.

"Where's Gareth?" she asked. "Has anybody seen Gareth lately?"

This proved to be a poser. One by one they looked at each other as if a proper reply belonged to someone other than themselves. Thomas topped up his glass and mused into the bubbles.

"I saw him a few weeks ago," he said. "He seemed a wee bit preoccupied...it was just before that *foo-fa-rah* in the harbour."

"What about that?" asked Andrew, looking pointedly at Nicholas and Brandywine.

"What about what, Andy?" replied Windy innocently.

"Well...you two were there...."

"We were...and then the newspapers wanted t'know what happened and we told them."

"We don't know anything else about it but it certainly was exciting wasn't it Windy?" Brandy added in one breath.

Nicholas nodded emphatically. "Very exciting. We enjoyed it immensely...and speaking of, Andy...where's that cute guy you've been hanging out with lately?"

Andrew blushed. "Alain's been working at the market beside the river on Water Street."

"He's actually employed?" said Thomas incredulously. "We need to fix that..."

"What about Gareth!" cried Diana.

"I told you, Di, I saw him a few weeks ago."

Once again they all looked to each other for illumination. This time Brandy fidgeted a little bit.

"I saw him last week...maybe," she said hesitantly.

"Either you did or you didn't, Brandy," snapped Diana. "What's it gonna be?"

"I promised I wouldn't say anything."

"Well it's a bit late now, isn't it?" observed Thomas, not unkindly.

Brandy looked at Andrew and Nicholas for moral support, but all they could do was shrug helplessly, having no insights of their own on the issue.

"We went to the animal park," she said quickly. "He asked me to make some drawings for him...and I'm not telling anything else, because I promised."

"Something funny is going on," said Diana emphatically. "Funny peculiar, not funny ha-ha."

Thomas said, "Andy, when do we get t'actually meet this guy Alain...?"

Windy ordered more wine.

The something funny going on had started a good ten days earlier than Thomas' recollection of having seen Gareth "a few weeks ago". The young man had tossed and turned through an entire night of restlessness brought on by nothing he could pinpoint with any accuracy, though he *had* partaken of a bit more than his share of some mouth-watering *hors d'oeuvres* at a *soiree* he had attended the previous evening.

Some time well before he was ready to greet the light of day, there had been a thunderous pounding on the doors of his stable/studio on Old Princes Street. He had padded the length of his digs, hopping into a pair of trousers on the way whilst attempting to negotiate an obstacle course of a dozen different chunks of stone, and tables bearing half-finished clay sculptures. When he had managed to swing one of the doors wide and stand blinking in the sunlight, someone in rough workman's clothing stood outside the door, a large horse-drawn cart behind him.

"Got a delivery for Gareth Davies," he said, consulting a clipboard. "You him?"

"I am," said Gareth.

"Sign here," said the someone, offering up the clipboard and indicating a line at the bottom of a delivery order.

"But I've not ordered anything for delivery," said Gareth, "and whatever it is, I'm sure I can't pay for it."

"I'm not gonna argue with you over this, buddy," said the deliveryman. "It says these here goods is supposed t'be delivered to Gareth Davies at this address, and besides, it's already paid for, exceptin' maybe a gratuity that I wouldn't be turnin' down if it was offered."

The faceless man looked over his shoulder at the good-sized wooden crate on his cart.

Gareth wandered out into the street and squinted at rows of characters in some language he'd never encountered before, though his name and address *were* plainly visible.

"I guess you're gonna need some help with this," he said.

The deliveryman grunted something that resembled *I could use a bit of help, though you're pretty scrawny so don't be hurtin' yerself...*

Together they wrestled the crate onto a wheeled contrivance and thence into Gareth's studio.

"It says here *THIS SIDE UP*," said Gareth, indicating some lettering and an arrow in the direction of where *up* should be.

"How d'you know that?"

"It says so."

"Where?"

"Right here," said Gareth, pointing.

"You can read that?"

Gareth looked again, and realised whatever it was he had taken to mean what he thought it meant was in the same strange script he hadn't understood before. It occurred to him that something funny was going on. Funny peculiar, not funny ha-ha...

With the right side up, he found a pry-bar beneath a work table and opened the crate carefully, his feet getting buried in tightly-packed straw that burst from inside once there was a prospect of outside. What he ended up with was a block of marble—as had been the case with the exterior markings of the crate—unlike any kind of stone he'd ever seen before.

It stood a little less tall and wide than himself, a roughly-hewn rectangular piece of stone in three dimensions, mostly a deep deep chocolate brown in colour, edging towards a rust-brown at the base, with heavy veins of white across the front face that swept backwards through the stone as they neared the floor. Gareth whistled appreciatively, found coffee and continued to marvel at it while the coffee got cold. He wondered where the marble itself had come from, and who might have sent it to him, but not for any great length of time, because those questions gradually floated away as he contemplated what he might actually *do* with such a unique piece of material.

At length it became problematical. Every possible project he conjured up in his mind just didn't seem to measure up to the exquisite colouring and veining of the stone. This went on for well over a week, which is when Thomas had encountered him, and found him a bit *preoccupied*. Then the dreams started, and thereafter Gareth unofficially went missing, until one morning another week later when he knocked on Brandy's door and requested her services at the animal park.

"Just a couple of hours, could you do that, Branny?" he had asked.

Branny could do that. She had a very difficult time ever turning down requests from her friends. When they got to the park it was crowded with children milling about in the nominal control of their schoolteachers, out for a field trip before the school term ended for the summer. She was delighted. Gareth seemed *preoccupied*. They went where he wandered; Brandy drew what was there when he pointed. When Brandy got curious about the motivation for *their* outing, Gareth apologetically declined to enlighten her.

Windy said, "I know you promised, Branny, but where did you go once you got there? What did he want you t'draw for him."

She looked at him beseechingly...said: "Foxes, Windy...he wanted me t'draw foxes for him please don't ask anymore..."

Gareth had never seen a desert, but when he got there he knew exactly what it was. He stood in the middle of a broad empty nowhere filled with nothing but sand gone gold and silver in the blistering heat of a north equatorial afternoon.

He decided to walk away from the sun, though before him rose up an immense mass of simmering sand shifting in a breeze come straight from the lowest level of Vulcan's basement. That he was stark bare-ass naked didn't seem to be a problem, though for a moment he gave some thought to the fairness of his skin, and wondered if a slumbering sunburn on your hinder parts would translate to some serious discomfort once one woke up. In the end it he decided he didn't care. He trudged up the side of the dune and when he got to the top found himself overlooking another broad basin similar to what he'd left behind, but this time with a ribbon of sun-struck diamonds running through it, and on the far side of the river, an ancient city.

That was when he noticed the foxes...

...And woke up to more pounding on the doors of his studio. Someone outside called to him by name, and he thought he recognised Tom Beverley's voice, but from where he lay propped up against his mysterious chunk of marble, he just didn't have what it took to get himself upright to find out for certain. The banging went on for a few more minutes, but Gareth was already off in Snoozeland...again...

They were there, all around him, at least a score of them, slinking and weaving their way through the sand, but always with their noses pointed in his direction and their eyes bright with a curious and somewhat unnerving awareness, as if they knew some great secret totally beyond his capabilities to understand, and were there to make sure he didn't mess things up too badly in his ignorance.

One of them seemed especially curious, and far less wary of him than the others. This one came within a dozen paces of him and would—in some odd but perfectly logical-seeming way—try to herd him in a specific direction every time he went stumbling off a direct route to the river below. He glowed in the sunlight, sparks of copper in his rust-red coat, the dark flicker at the end of his tail.

Gareth felt compelled to follow him, even as what lay below seemed to swim in his sight and become a series of overlapping kaleidoscopic images that encompassed the city glistening in the shimmer of a desert mirage along with what felt like an auditory collage of movement, the sound of bare feet skipping along marble hallways, voices lifted in songs sung in languages long gone from the earth.

His foxy entourage led him down to the river, to a small coracle woven from reeds lining the water, that appeared to be there waiting just for him. He steadied the small boat with his hands as he crept into it. The dog-fox was already there...waiting...his button eyes gleaming...his nose and whiskers twitching over what Gareth swore was a grin...

Thomas lounged just outside the doorway of Windy's house in the Mews, nursing an ale chilled so perfectly that tiny ice crystals dissolved the moment they hit his tongue. Beside him in another sling chair Diana sprawled in the summer sun, her long legs bare of dancer's tights, growing a bit brown in the sun. Windy arrived with her glass of *chauvignon*, plunked himself down in a third chair and awaited developments.

"He didn't answer," said Thomas. "Or maybe he just wasn't there at all, whisked away by some efreet or djinn recently arrived on our shores from the mystical marges of Araby."

"How poetical of you, Tom," said Diana. "You've been taking lessons from Andy..."

"What'd I say?" said Beverley.

Windy said, "You spoke of efreets and djinns and intimated the presence of influences from the immensity of far-off desert landscapes."

"Is that what I did?"

"Unquestionably," nodded Diana.

Beverley shook his head and swallowed half his glass at once.

"I have no idea. All I know is as I stood there waiting for no one to answer my shouting or pounding, I distinctly felt this dry parched wind rush down Old Princes Street, and found my nose up in the midst of spice and magic..."

Windy grinned. "You just let me know when you want another of those ales, Thomas."

Diana said, "Shouldn't we be concerned?"

Tom and Windy looked at each other.

"I suppose maybe we should," said Windy.

Gareth stepped gingerly from his craft, onto a small wooden quay thrust politely into the slow stream of the river's pilgrimage to the sea, wherever and whatever it might be. From there he found himself on a broad boulevard of interlocking sandstone pavers that varied in shades of rose and pink to pale-almost-white, bleached in the sun. Before him rose up a seemingly endless arcade flanked by pillars crowned with the images of every living creature imaginable...including foxes...

Magically, he had acquired long flowing robes of some silken white cloth through the fibres of which came a soft breeze off the river, redolent with the scents of spice and the promise of secrets revealed and wishes come true. He stopped briefly, thought to hear the faint echo of voices accompanying him, and the strains of musical instruments—a quiet thrumming of *tars*, the twang of single-stringed *rababas*, the lilting rhythms of *ouds* and *kissars*.

The dog-fox led him on, loping ahead of him, stopping to look over his shoulder when Gareth lagged behind. As he walked along the arcade, shaded now as well by tall date palms and fronded greenery that lifted up large white flowers with crimson hearts that dipped down to shower his way with sweet perfume, Gareth could swear to glimpses of bare-legged serving girls in glowing white *chitons*, brief trills of laughter, the hint of something invisible...long gone but waiting to be reborn.

He walked beneath an arched entryway, flanked by images of fox and leaf, walls painted in arabesques of deep blue, crimson and gold, sandstone giving way to glazed mosaic floors, tapestried walls, furnishings of intricately-carved cedar and rosewood.

Gareth sank into one of the scrolled armchairs, found a small tabouret beside him, a ewer and crystal goblet beside it. Beyond them the dog-fox dipped his head, inviting him to drink.

The water was icy cold...sweet...dizzying...

He woke up suddenly, aware there was someone close by, shaking him gently and calling him by name. He opened his eyes and looked into the concerned face of someone he'd never seen before.

"You're Gareth, aren't you?" asked the young man softly. "Andy's told me about you...all his friends..."

Gareth nodded yes and then shook his head to clear away proverbial cobwebs.

"Andrew McKinnon?" he mumbled. "Where are we?"

"Near the market by the river," said the young man. "I saw you asleep here on this bench and thought you had to be the Gareth who was Andy's friend. He described you perfectly."

"So who are you?"

"My name's Alain."

"How d'you know Andy?"

Alain stepped back a pace, to where Gareth could see him more clearly, in many ways almost a mirror image of Andrew, though neither so dark-haired nor pale-skinned.

"I met him a little while ago...we were reading poetry...he was with this beautiful little blonde girl..."

"Brandywine?"

Alain nodded. "That was her name, yes. Are you okay? Is it safe t'sleep on benches in the middle of the day? I'm still relatively new here. Where I'm from it's not something one does...as a rule...sleeping on benches ...y'know...?"

"You and Andy are seeing each other?"

"He said he was staying with...Windy? he said...but felt a bit badly about it and wanted a place of his own... but I had more room than I needed and...well...we talked forever the day after I met him at the reading with Brandywine and he was quite lovely so..."

Gareth nodded and tottered up onto his feet.

"He is...he's better than just lovely...all of them are I guess you'll get to meet them soon." He consulted a pocket-watch, that looped into a pocket of his trousers on a thin gold chain.

"But I've really got t'be going..."

"Are you okay?" Alain asked again.

Gareth's eyes got cloudy with a dream...

"Sure," he said, moving off down the street. "Nice t'have met you..."

Alain watched him go. "Yeah me too," he said to Gareth's receding figure.

He realised he had come to a palace of sorts, cool in spite of the heat outside, forever echoing with intimations of what might have lived and breathed in the shelter of its walls.

He drained his goblet, poured himself another, intoxicated by its sweetness, suddenly feeling as though his surroundings had leapt into a new clarity, a greater brightness than the moment before. The place seemed to be more *alive* with his presence, as if centuries had gone by waiting for him to arrive.

He stood again, and the dog-fox leapt before him, tugged briefly at the hem of his robes and led him out of the entrance hall, down a corridor painted with almost-cuneic characters that felt vaguely familiar to him, and figures that told a story of some sort that he felt certain he had known at one time or another.

The claws of the fox skittered softly on marble flooring as he led Gareth deeper into the interior of the palace...

Alain went home to Andrew and recounted his encounter with the snoozified stranger he had supposed, quite rightly, to be Gareth.

"There was a pocket-watch?" inquired Andy.

"There was!" exclaimed Alain.

"That was Gareth, all right. Y'know that thing has never told the time in all the time Gareth's owned it...but what was he doing on Water Street...?

"Sleeping on a bench in the middle of the day."

"Diana was right," said Andrew. "Something funny's going on..."

"Funny peculiar, not funny ha-ha?" asked Alain, and Andy looked at him with a different kind of funny.

"I think we need to get everyone together and find out what he's up to," he said.

They did...for three days running...and on the fourth day *les Boulevardiers*-minus-one once again stood outside the doors of Gareth's stable/studio on Old Princes Street, having knocked with no response for five minutes.

"He's in there, for sure," observed Windy. "I can hear him banging away at something. He's been at it all week"

"Try knocking again, Thomas," suggested Brandy. "Maybe he didn't hear you."

Diana got huffy. "Of course he heard," she said with a tinge of asperity. "Thomas near knocked the doors down entirely."

Brandy appeared chastened, but unwilling to think ill of their friend. "Well it's just not like him to ignore us like this. Maybe he's not feeling well."

"He's well enough to be smashing away at something in there," offered Tom.

Alain piped up, but quietly, having only just met everyone and still feeling like he hadn't yet really become one of them.

"He's being creative."

That seemed to sum things up nicely. They stood away from the doors in a small group, ignoring the attentions of passersby, looking at each other until Alain again piped up:

"Maybe we should just let him go on? Don't want to mess things up with his Muse-for-a-day?"

Windy grinned at Alain. Alain grinned back. Andrew blushed with something that could have been mistaken for warm pride, and Brandy hugged them both, feeling entitled to do so as having been witness to their discovery of each other. Diana sighed and suggested any further review of the situation would best be served by refreshments on the terrace of the Silver Rose. Thomas concurred with a great deal of enthusiasm.

Some time within the next few days, Gareth awoke as if from some long, deep and uninterrupted sleep, dozy with dreams and for the first few minutes of his newly-resumed consciousness, unable to understand why he lay on the floor of his studio with the dusty spice of desert sand in his nostrils, and the sand itself in corners of his clothing where it had no right to be. He raised himself off the floor woozily, looked around, and realised he lay in the shadow of a sculpture he could not recall having had anything to do with, though he recognised it as the finished product of the mysterious block of marble that had been delivered to his door. He breathed a sigh of relief when he saw the bottle of wine on the floor beside it, but then realised the bottle had never been opened.

He was left with no explanations for anything, especially when, looking up at the sculpture, he was struck with an intense almost painful attraction, a desperate longing for the delicious vision in stone before him—a slender chocolate-brown girl in a loose-fitting gown of white, who seemed to sway like river reeds, her face mischievous with joy, wreathed in a halo of dark curls, her almost-dancing legs caressed by a russet-brown dog-fox who gamboled at her feet.

His fascination and bewitchment were interrupted by someone knocking on the doors of his stable and in his mind there came a thought...

Not again...

...But he staggered up onto his feet and once again made his way through the obstacle course of his studio...undid the latches on the doors...swung them wide and stood blinking in late afternoon sunlight...at a slender chocolate-brown girl in a loose-fitting gown of white, who seemed to sway like river reeds, her face mischievous with joy, wreathed in a halo of dark curls,

"Oh," she breathed, "you are lovely."

She reached forward and handed to him the grinning dog-fox held in her arms.

"You know Hasan. I am Zoraya...there was an evil sorcerer..."

He followed her back into the stables, directly to where the statue...had been...for now there was nothing but a heap of chocolate marble dust that now and again gleamed russet brown or porcelain white. When she turned to him her smile was radiant.

"I knew you would be the one. I could not be free again until someone saw me."

Under a Mauve-Grey Moon

He stood among the shadows at the edge of the New City, at the foot of one of the tall glass-and-steel office towers that rose up into the black-velvet-and-fleece night sky, dark and quiet now that its small army of workers had gone home to hot suppers and warm beds, and fireplaces crackling with orange-dancing flames to ward off the sudden chill of autumn in the air.

He could taste the crisp scent of stiffening leaves turned crimson, yellow and brown; his nostrils twitched at the familiar smell, his lips curving in a kindly but very cryptic-seeming smile. The air was becoming near-wintry and the shadows grew deeper and deeper with each passing day, but autumn had always been that way. He had lived long enough to know that, to become accustomed to the quickening flight of daylight, the keen shadow-edge of twilight, the cool crystal clarity of the night itself. He had lived long enough to recognise the signs of summer's end, and the world's slow fall into winter dreaming...

All of this was familiar to him, easily accepted as something that was, after all, no more and no less than the way of things; however if there was any sadness in his soul at the passing of summer—the slow round of heat-drowsy days into the swift coolth of the sleep seasons—it was banished now by the very specialness of the night before him, a night unquestionably destined to become a milestone in his life...full with improbable happenings of a wondrous nature.

His gaze went up and up into the sky, unwinking eyes climbing the steel spires of the City to the rare and splendid miracle of the moon, where it floated amid wreaths and wisps of cloud-cotton...full and bright... tinged with the faintest hint of violet...

He had seen the golden glory of countless Harvest moons, and the smouldering of many a dark and crimson Devil's moon, but never in his experience had there been such a moon as the one that ruled the heavens tonight. It was a thing of legend, spoken of in hushed tones of awe and wonder, a thing so uncommon that in his ken, only an aged grandmother had ever seen one...a mauve-grey moon...

"...I'll never forget that night, my little wean," his *grand-mère* once had told him when he was very small. "From sunrise to sunset the whole City fairly hummed with a blind sort of excitement, knowing something was in the wind but not quite certain of what it might be. The Wheel had turned quickly that year, and ragged bits of snow had been seen far up in the north corners of the town early on that morning...but when the darkness came down there wasn't a cloud to be seen in the sky, and when the moon came up...well...the leafs started in to dancing and the hounds started in to howling and there was nary a nose in the realm couldn't smell Magick in the air..."

And now he stood in the light of the magic moon, moving slowly and softly in the merest whisper of a breeze that wafted down the deserted streets; and he could hear the faraway howling of the hounds and the dancing of the leaves, feel the throb of excitement in all who lived and breathed in the essence of the magical night. Again, the words of his grandmother came to him:

"...We all wondered who would be the one to walk the Way of the Witch that night," she had said. "Who would be the Chosen One, to rise up in a shower of stars and wear the Witch-crown...and we waited, my little wean, oh but we waited...breathless we was through half the night..."

And here it was that his grandmother had made the warm chuckling sound in her throat, and grinned so widely he had feared the kind old whiskery face would grin itself apart...

"You'd not know t'look at her now, my wee scamp, but it was your own first cousin Tabitha's granny who was Chosen...and what a sight she was, I can tell you! She was a real beauty then—I don't think there was one among us who didn't act like the randiest old tom-cat where she was concerned—but that night we learned what more-than-beauty looked like...and saw with our own eyes the power of the Old Magick..."

The Old Magick. That had lived long before there was ever a City, when even his family, older than old, was like a newborn wean just birthed from the womb of the world. And he smiled again, striding quickly now in the mauve-grey moonlight, bathing in it, full with the knowledge that the Old Magick had touched him...alive and well...that the dream had become a reality and it was *his* night to wear the crown of stars, to walk the Witch's Way...

And what shall I do this night? he asked himself. *What wonders shall I work, what prodigies of Nature shall spring up in my path...*

These thoughts brought memory of another time, when he had dared to approach Tabitha's grandmother, and spoken with her...

"You have nothing to do but walk on such a night," she had replied to his shy questions.

"Nothing to do but what *you* would have done. The Magick is in the walking, and the Witch's Way is wherever *you* would go..."

And so he walked, and went his way as he would have gone on any other night, a tall slender figure grey-cloaked and grey-clad, with boots of grey leather on his feet and moonbeams dancing on the silk-fine grey of his hair...young as he could feel...moving silently through the City until he came to a small house that seemed out of place amongst its taller neighbours, where a square of light shone brightly in a third-storey garret window.

"She works late tonight," he said aloud, marveling at the sound of his voice, conjuring in his mind the image of the girl who lived there, whose hair was the colour of honey in sunlight and whose skin was golden brown and soft with rich round curves. "Her legs are crossed and she sings to herself as she works, making pictures on squares of white paper, her eyes wide and green as a cat's, that see only the Magick and how she can make it come alive..."

And she is well and happy tonight, this girl of sunshine named Brandy, needing no comfort from me...

So he continued on his rounds, knowing his next destination would be something of an adventure, because the young man who lived there had not done so for any great length of time, and his own unerring sense of direction had yet to become familiar with the surrounding neighbourhood of the Old City.

But I am Magick tonight! he told himself, *and there is nowhere I cannot go!*

And for the first time ever he was able to find his way to the tiny basement apartment with trouble at all...turning left where Grail Street met with Blackthorn Lane, left again onto Crescent Street and then right with a twist and a wriggle, into the alley beside the Jolly Beggar public house on *Rue de l'Espoir*, where, halfway to the falling-down fence at the end of the alley, a thin rectangle of flickering light shone but a few inches from the ground.

"Another one who lingers at his work," he said, shaking his head ruefully. "The pale young man with the black hair and midnight eyes, who has only just found Love and, making word-songs with his pen, would share it with the world..."

He peered cautiously through the window, down into a sparsely-furnished room where the poet sat at his candle-lit table with a quill in his hand, seeking after the mystery of expressing Joy, agonising with each word, watering the parchment wasteland before him with its tears and its Hope, wrestling with his soul that he might convert the measure of his newfound happiness into rhymes and meters that others could share.

In his heart he yet suffers, does this one, the memory of it still too bright...but he is cautious by nature...it is his way...a child seeking Light... and I am not the one to disturb him, for the hurt has been the anvil of his art, whereon he becomes the Man rather than the boy, and forges the shape and the character of his truths...

Another figure came to stand beside the poet, bent to kiss him...and then he was gone, with a swirl of his grey cloak, a swift but silent patter of his boots upon the floor of the alley, and a bounding leap up and over the fence, dashing the length of King Willem's Road until the broad lamplit ribbon of the Boulevard unfolded before him and he was back in familiar territory...with moonlight flashing at his heels and the stars in a dizzy whirl about his head...he laughed joyously...uncaring of those who, in motor cars on the Boulevard, stared out at him with incredulous eyes...seeing Magick...but never knowing it was Magick they saw...

He came to an archway of stone he knew very well, flanked on one side as it was by the grounds of the church, and then the cobbled laneway and courtyard.

And here I shall find Nicholas...the tall sun-child who makes such music that all who pass must stop to listen...dream his dreams...hear the heartbeat of the City...

He crept softly along the cobblestones, in darkness rich with the smell of late bloom roses and the lingering scent of the apple trees that ringed the courtyard ahead...then back into moonlight. He looked up to the second-floor window of the musician's house and heard silvery pure notes, coaxed by a pair of loving hands on the strings of a harp...out into the night, to play a child's game of hide-and-seek with the wind.

His feet slowed and hesitated, then stopped as he cocked his head to one side and his ears strained to the music that slowly, with each passing day, took on the strength and subtle harmonies that soon would make it complete. And then, in nodding great satisfaction to himself, he realised he was not alone in the courtyard; that while Nicholas bent his winter-pale head of long hair over his harp, dozens of furred shapes filled the branches of the trees, sat unmoving atop the wall enclosing the courtyard, and twice a dozen of unwinking eyes stared up at his window...while they listened...

"Good evening to you, sweet kitten-bundle," he whispered to the small black-and-silver tabby who sat, with tiny paws tucked beneath her chest, on a wooden bench close by. The little lamps of her eyes grew wide with wonder as he came to sit beside her, bent his head to kiss her between the ears. "You are so very small and so very blest to see this moon on this night, and come here to listen, to dream of the wild Green Lands where the skies are filled with low-flying slow-flying birds to tease you out into the fields..."

The kitten licked his hand once, where an amethyst stone set in silver encircled one finger, and shone with a light to mirror the moon overhead. He smiled, crooked that finger beneath her chin, felt the tiny body begin to vibrate with a rumbling purr of delight.

Sit and dream he said to them all. *I've heard his music before; he is well and I must be on my way...*

He rose and followed the breeze back out to the Boulevard, glancing up at the moon to be certain there was and time enough for him yet to finish his rounds as he went lightly past the iron scrollwork fence standing as the outermost defense of the Defender's church. Inside, he knew that a round ball of a priest—Ambrosius he was named—lay fast in deep slumber, dreaming his own dreams of one god and a multitude of saints.

Perhaps one god would be a wondrous fine thought if everyone would think of the same one. Perhaps he seeks a one god more kindly then the one he has known...

Bu he had neither the time nor much inclination to dwell upon such things. Ambrosius could look after that for himself. He began to move so quickly that his cloak became as wings, and his feet scarcely to touch upon the pavement beneath them. He hurried on up the Boulevard, past the Café of the Silver Rose, where those upon its sidewalk terrace drank tall tulip glasses of amber wine and, all unwitting, mixed it with mauve-grey moonlight and thereby drank of the Old Magick each time they raised them to their lips.

Heigh and ho! he cried to them silently. *May the god of your choice treat you well and leave light in your eyes...*

He danced past the entrance to the Emerald Gardens, pranced and capered before the gates of the Amaranth Palace and raced the length of the West Abbey Road until he came to Boar's Head Lane and dared to parade himself in front of the lair of the great bear named Thomas...

"Yes...there's his window...half-open as well," he observed aloud. "And within he sits, broad back hunched over his foolscap while he attacks it with the fang-and-claw of his pen, making razor sharp mockery of his own foolishness, all the while seeking Truth..."

Suddenly the silence of the lane was broken by a muffled oath, the angry shriek of a chair thrust back from its table, and then a crumpled ball of foolscap shot through the half-open window to tumble at his feet...or where his feet had been...for he already had moved on, leaving a faint echo of laughter in reply to the writer's snort of frustration. He strode on through the night breathing deeply of the crisp dripping-with-moonlight air, seeking a wide cobbled court that opened directly onto Old Princes Street, where an old prince's stable was set back from the road...

And here is the flame-haired godling, who hammers away at his monuments to Life with the passion of a lover yearning for his Love, and the will to free them from their prisons of stone.

At the closed doors of the stable he set one ear to the weather-worn planks, and from the silence drew mnemonic memory of chisels and hammers and gouges creating form from wood and stone.

This one is up to something, of a certainty, though now his forge is dark. Will you fashion a goddess for Ambrosius he asked quietly. *Perhaps a faun to grace a walk in the Emerald Gardens by day...and dance them all by night? Ah, Sieur Gareth, never was there a Titan so great as thee, for all thy stature's brevity...and then, of course, the dusky princess...*

And he was gone again, swift as thought, with one more in his mind that the rest of this magic night might belong to him alone...and with that there left him all sense of urgency and his footsteps slowed to jaunty stroll.

The Magick is in the walking, and the Witch's Way is wherever I would go...

"...Her name is Diana...the Huntress...Moon-goddess... and it is only fitting and proper that she should be the last I see safe and sound on this night..."

But as he turned on the street that faced the rear of where she lived in the long studio loft with its walls of moon-silvered glass and mirror images, he knew, even without closer inspection of the trice of darkened windows above him, that she, out of all his self-appointed wards, was not safe and sound at home; that she was somewhere out and about in the City, and there would be neither rest nor wild abandon for him until such time as he could find her and see to the serenity of her night's rest.

For the first time that evening, ever since he had been touched by the Magick and begun his tour of the City, he stood perfectly still, one hand poised in mid-air before him as if he might, with but a word and some arcane gesture, materialise her before him.

"Plaintively he cried, "But the Magick will not go that far...and I cannot rest if I cannot find her..."

Some inner sense told him that this was as it was meant to be; that he had been Chosen that he might find her gone, and in that finding seek her out...that she needed to be found by him...under a mauve-grey moon...so that the turning of the Wheel could bring only good things to her door.

But where...? he asked himself. *And what shall I do...having found her how shall I know what is right? Can I...dare I speak to her, never having spoken before?*

He trembled at the enormity of the task set suddenly before him, yet resolved in that same instant it would be done. The urgency that had left him now returned doubled and trebled, for he could not know how long his search would take...and if the moon was gone...with his task undone...?

He shook his head, banishing such a thought as unthinkable, and became a blur of motion, a shadow-wraith of violet and grey light.

His quest took him across the City at a frantic pace as he visited every place he ever had known her to frequent...at any time...for any reason. He retraced his steps to the Silver Rose Café...sought vainly her face amongst those who yet lingered over their amber- wine-and-moonlight...fairly flew to the hall where her dance company practised each evening and found them dark and deserted...and thence again to the Gardens...the Palace grounds...the Promenade beside the harbour...the zoological park where the great hunting cats dozed and dreamed of Freedom....among the ruins of the Armoury...and failed in every place to catch even a whisper of her recent presence anywhere...

...Until he came at length to the canal, and there, as he walked disconsolately along its railed embankments, he saw her sitting alone...on a wooden bench not far from King Stephen's Bridge...staring sightlessly at the rectangle of paper she held in one hand, heedless of his footsteps as he approached her.

She is crying! he thought with horror. *On such a night as this she is crying...!*

The heartrending immensity of this drew him towards her much more quickly than he had intended, brought him to within a handful of paces and...left him there...trembling in every inch of himself...looking down at her glossy cap of close-cropped hair...

"Diana you musn't cry," he said softly, more frightened than he had ever been in his life.

"Go away!" she answered him. "Leave me alone!" she sobbed, without looking up; and then, realising she had heard herself spoken to by name, turned to him wildly, her tears like tragic jewels in the moonlight, splattered across her face.

"Who are you?" she demanded brokenly. "How do you know my name when I have never seen you before?"

She blinked through her tears, saw him clearly for the first time—a tall willow-slender man of perhaps twice her own age, dressed all in grey down to his very shirt, staring down at her with bright green eyes that shone forth from a finely-boned face framed by silver-grey hair...seemingly crowned by the stars that wheeled above them in the night sky.

"Who are you?" she asked again, and strangely, she felt no fear of this stranger though the hour was late, the embankments of the canal deserted. "Have we met...?"

He sensed her cautious acceptance in the lessening of tension in her body, ventured an equally cautious smile while his brain worked feverishly for an answer to her question.

"I do not think we have ever met...formally..." he said slowly, "but I know you very well...I mean...I have seen you dance...many times...heard your name. You are a marvelous dancer...you know that, of course..."

She nodded once, almost imperceptibly, at his compliment, but then he saw the pain return to her eyes, a fresh welling of tears that spilled onto her cheeks as she quickly turned away from him.

"Please..." he said. "I was walking and I saw you...recognised your face, heard you crying..."

He stopped again unsure of what next he might say to her.

"If there is anything I can do to ease your hurt...?"

She shook her head, refusing to look at him.

"There's nothing you can do...thank you..." she whispered, and the anguish in her voice tore at his heart.

"But I must!" he cried, and when she looked up at him again, imperious through her tears that he should dare to insist, he added hastily, "I mean...I cannot just leave you here... like this...not on such a night...when the moon—"

"Who are you?" she asked a third time, and now the Magick dictated he must in some way reply to her thrice-posed question, else it would desert him.

"You may call me Grey," he said softly. "Most everyone does...for obvious reasons..."

"And why *must* you offer me assistance?" she pressed him.

"Because I have seen you dance, Diana," he replied. "Because your dancing has given me pleasure and joy...and I can repay you in no other way than this—to try to stand between you and whatever it is that has given you so much pain. May I...sit...?"

She looked up into his face, gazed into his wide green eyes, saw in them what was, perhaps, a reflection of her own inner torment...and relented...acceded to his request with a slight inclination of her head.

"Will you tell me what is troubling you?" he asked gently, watching her long-fingered hands clutch at the paper they held until the veins beneath her skin stood out in dark tracery.

"No...no...it's something personal," she sobbed, closing here eyes. "I can't talk...it's very kind of you, but..."

"I am a friend, Diana," he said. "We've never truly met before this night, but I *am* your friend..."

He sensed the struggle his words precipitated within her—the need to unburden herself to *someone*. She was dressed as he always had seen her—in black dancer's tights, slippers, a light fashionably-ragged overdress—and now she began to shiver in the damp chill rising up off the canal...and his hands went to her without thinking he glimpsed the sudden doe-like terror in her eyes as her head jerked around to face him...one hand...that held the paper...rising in reflex...and stopping midway between them as she saw...or perhaps felt...the honesty of his concern.

"It's my mother," she said hoarsely. "Oh God...my mum's dead...she's been sick I was going t'go home...but she died, Grey...she died yesterday and now...now I'll never see her again..."

And then she let herself be folded into his arms, flooding the front of his shirt with her tears as he stroked the cap of her hair, so much like the coat of a short-haired cat in its startling softness.

"How else should it be? he asked himself. *She is so much like a cat...sleek and lovely, her dancing wild and exquisite...but her grief...so great as not to be borne by any living thing...*

"You cannot blame yourself," he said gently. "It's the way of things...like the changing of the seasons..."

"But you don't understand!" she cried, shaking her head as she clung to him even more tightly. "There was so much I meant to tell her, so many things I should have said and shared and now it's too late. I'll never be able to tell her how much I love her...or thank her for giving me so much...

"She could've been a dancer herself. She was so strong, so beautiful...and my father wanted to bring her back to the City...so she could study and learn...but when she became pregnant with me she said that she wanted me more than anything else in the world, and then my father died in a storm...the love of her life...

"When I was growing up, I watched her dance through all the things she did—cleaning our house, making suppers, doing the washing and taking work to help meet our expenses—I told her I wanted to be a dancer just like her..."

She drew her head up and looked into his eyes, her face twisted with grief and the pain of remembering.

"She said, *No Diana you will not be a dancer just like me, because I chose not be a dancer at all...but you* will *be, my sweet girl...that much I will promise you, and you will dance enough for the both of us...*

"And she kept her promise, even after my father was lost in the ocean she kept her promise to me, working at any job she could find, saving every copper so that someday I could come here. She went in rags for me! She denied herself everything ..."

"But that was her choice, Diana," he said, brushing tears from her cheeks with his fingertips. "It would not have been that way if she had wanted it otherwise. She loved you—"

"But it killed her, Grey. I killed her! She worked too hard, kept sending me money, even after I began to earn money on my own...and I never *really* thanked her, never really told her how much I appreciated what she had done. Grey, she saw me dance once! What kind of payment was that for all the things she had given up for me...?"

He looked up into the sky, where a mauve-grey moon floated on the tides of an ocean far greater than anything that had ever been or would be, and realised the nature and purpose of that which had made him the Chosen One on this night.

"Diana, I must tell you something now and you must listen," he said. "You must listen to me, and not allow this thing to undo everything your mother worked so hard for. It is something that has been known to my family for years and years, ever since the first of my kind came to be here, and that was long before this place even existed...

"We have known so much Death, Diana—in a family so old how could we not?—and we learned quickly that no one of us would be spared, that Death was all we could ever hope for as an end to our lives...and we learned as well that when Death claimed one of us, it was Life telling us that our work among the living was complete; that She who rules over all things had need of that soul for some other work—"

"But she's dead!" sobbed Diana. "I could've told her...said something...anything...but I was always too busy becoming a dancer, and dripping with pride because I was so good at it..."

He smiled at her, sadly, wiped away more tears, brought her back into his arms.

"We learned something else," he said, "and simply, it was this—that when someone close to us was taken, there always would be words and thoughts left unspoken, acts of love and kindness undone; that the tears we shed over another's passing were an expression of our own fear and unhappiness at having been left alive to grieve...alone...seemingly deserted by the one who had died...and for that reason we made a Night of Tears, where all the words and thoughts could be spoken aloud and our Peace made with the one who was gone."

She shuddered in his arms, shaking her head.

"What difference can it make?" she cried bitterly. "When people die they're dead, they don't listen anymore...they can't hear—"

"But they can, Diana," he said urgently, taking her face in his hands and staring into her eyes. "They can hear us! I will tell you how I know, and you will see that I'm right.

"When we die we become dust, and the dust of what we have been returns to what it always has been, to become something else that lives. How can it be otherwise? In every tiny bit of flesh and bone that comes together to make us alive, there is an essence of Life, a spark, a glimmer of something that is the *power* to make Life. The universe is a great ever-boiling cauldron of these sparks, a place where one thing dies and another springs into being to replace it. Your mother as you have known her is gone from you, but she is here beside us even now, gone back into the cauldron of the universe and, for a time, will be part of everything that exists, until she becomes part of something or someone else... but if you cannot speak to her now, say and feel all the things you wish you could have said and felt when she was the mother you knew and recognised, then she will be bound here...to you...and unable to go on.

"She will be bound for so long as your grief and tears are alive within you...and that is the reason for the Night of Tears, whether it be a moment, an hour, a day, or a month in coming."

"How can you know?" she asked. "How can you be certain...?"

She looked at him, her dark eyes disbelieving, but pleading with him for some word or thought that would allow *her* to believe...and he looked at her, felt a sudden rush of power rising up within him that was the Magick of the night.

"I know," Diana," he whispered, suddenly near speechless himself with revelation. "I am certain..."

"She'll hear me?" the girl whispered back. "If I say how much I love her, thank her for everything, for loving me enough to give me what she chose not to give to herself...she'll know...?"

"And be free," he nodded slowly, willing all the Magick inside him to come together in a certainty of *her* own fashioning. "Speak to her now...aloud...in thought...it doesn't matter she will hear you...but say all the things you want to say if you had known...if there had been one more day with her..."

He stood slowly, drew her up beside him.

"Come, I'll walk with you...try to help you see her in the stars, in the trees, the stones beneath your feet, in the song of sparrows singing to celebrate the end of your Night of Tears, and the flight of your mother's soul back to the Beginning."

They stood together—his arm about her shoulders and hers about his waist—and began to walk along the canal that way, in silence, listening to the whisper of the water flowing by beside them, the wind rustling through trees already beginning to dream of their rebirth on the far side of winter.

At length she drew apart from him, until he held only her hand in his own, could see her cheeks still bright with tears and moonlight, and her lips moving soundlessly...they walked...past King Stephen's Bridge...the Bridge of Sighs...where the water's voice spoke to them both of Joy and of Sorrow, loss and redemption...and then on to the bell towers of Queen Iolanthe where high above them stone angels stood silently against the night sky and kept watch upon the City...she whispered softly...

"Thank you, mum...for everything. I love you."

...And turned to him, her hands aimlessly fluttering about her clothing for a handkerchief he drew from the folds of his own cloak.

"Did you say all?" he asked, taking the cloak from his own shoulders to drape it over hers.

"Yes," she said, wiping her eyes and her cheeks. "Did she—?"

"Yes, she did," he smiled, "and all the world heard you as well. Can you believe that now?"

She nodded, drew his cloak more tightly around her, shivering slightly.

"I do," she whispered. "I thought I heard her voice, telling me she never once doubted me...that every dance will forever be the measure of my love for her.

"Grey, she *did* hear me! You were right...how can I thank you...?"

"You will let me walk you home, see you safely to your door," he said. "I ask that for myself. You cannot thank me for a Truth that has always belonged to you."

"I never would have known...I would've cried for her forever...never allowed her to go free..."

"I did only what I was meant to do," he replied, and looked over her shoulder, to where the moon had begun to glow ever more brightly in the western sky...

They stood before the door that opened onto the flight of stairs leading up to her loft, as she searched for her keys in a small pouch she wore belted about her waist. When the door was half-open and her hand yet upon the latch, she turned back to him and he saw her face had lost its expression of ungovernable loss, wore instead a look of quietness and peace.

"Will you come up with me?" she asked. "A cup of tea...before you go...?"

He felt himself trembling as she returned his cloak, as he first had trembled to speak to her...suddenly unsure of what he should do...how he should behave...

"Please," she urged him. "It's very late, but you've done so much for me and I know... somehow...this is the only night that will be for us..."

She took his hand, drew him through the doorway and led him up the dark stair to another door that she unlocked with another key, flinging it wide upon a long room with a polished wooden floor that shone in the ghostly light flooding through the trice of windows in the opposite wall, and then again on the mirrored wall to his left. At the far end of the loft he could see a curtained archway into a small kitchen area, and beyond that a smaller alcove of the bathroom. A series of painted screens—dancers in silhouette—hid her bed, a wooden desk and a shelf of books.

Brandy's work...a gift to her friend...

"Please come in," she said. "I really haven't gotten round to real furniture, but we can sit on my bed...or on the floor...just for a little while..."

The Magick is so strong here he thought, as they crossed the empty floor that was aglow with moonlight, watched their reflections in the endless mirrors. *I cannot stay here...not for long...or I shall melt in it...*

But he spread his cloak on the floor while she made tea in a china pot, stared at himself in the mirrors as he waited...full with wonder to see what the Magick had made of him... what he had made of her when she came...finally...to sit beside him.

"You were looking for me, weren't you?" she asked softly, as she poured their tea into small mugs.

He nodded once. "But you mustn't ask me why, for I hardly know the answer to that myself. It was the moon..."

He looked through her wall of windows, that overlooked the roof of a low house on the next street, and saw it in the sky, still round in violet and grey, floating peacefully down the night sky drawing the new day after it on invisible strings. When he turned back to her, she too was staring out the windows...

"Is she gone, Grey? Could I...would she know now...if I were to dance for her...?"

"She will always know, Diana," he breathed.

She rose in one sinuous movement that seemed effortless—as if suddenly she were as light as a feather floating on the moonbeams that filled her loft—and walked slowly to the centre of the room to stand there, utterly still save for the rise and fall of her breast as she relaxed her breathing, looked inwardly to her heart and soul. She moved one foot tentatively, followed it with another step, whirled slowly and then leapt into the air... once...landing without a sound...crouching now with her fingertips on the floor...came up again and moved in a slow arabesque...to some music only she could hear...

He watched her become an unborn child, come forth from her mother's womb and grow...awkwardly at first...but with the passage of Time enriched by her mother's love and care...becoming taller and stronger with her mother's promise to her coming to fulfillment...until she was fully grown...confident now in her Art...each movement a song unto itself...a word of Love and unfailing Memory come to a night of mauve-grey moonlight, where she beckoned to a stranger...

"Dance with me, Grey," she called to him silently, and he rose up to join her, knowing miraculously each step, every caress as she drew them along, from light into darkness and shadow and back again into light...again and again he felt they had danced for hours she heard him whisper:

"Now for farewells..."

And they were caught in a whirlwind of what they fashioned as a final gift. She saw him become a grey blur of her own thought/music/love in complement to her own image... leaping away...dancing the song of her mother's passing...she ached...called for him/her to return...pursued him...cried in agony as she came to the borderlands of Life and Death and she could go no further...grief-struck...embraced...solaced...the farewell:

G'bye, mum...

And became still again, her right hand outstretched, looking back over her shoulder along the length of her left arm where her fingertips were joined to his...in fact...in the mirror where she *saw* his fingers touching her own...and beyond them a mauve-grey moon slipping down into the west for a moment she saw him crowned with stars...

And then he was gone with the moon. As she turned to look for him, calling for him in a voice that seemed to echo with every warmth in the world...she saw a grey blur moving towards the door she had left half-open...and a brief flash of green cat's-eyes...

Tristesse

Windy went walking. There was a vast sense of relief and accomplishment in his thoughts. Relief for having finished the symphony, something he had dreamed of for years, never feeling himself capable or worthy of creating anything on such a scale; the sense of accomplishment come in its thunderous reception by the select audience who had been there for its introduction to the world.

But in the aftermath of the performance he had wept through most of the night, overwrought and thoroughly exhausted, humbled by the knowledge that something of his soul had been received with any kind of welcome. He wondered how it must have been for Beethoven—unable to hear any kind of music at all but for what it sounded like in his head—on a spring day in May 1824 when the *Ode to Joy* had roused the Viennese to their feet, overwhelmed, in tears and laughter, stunned by the magnitude of a lunatic's vision of redemption and beauty.

The City thrummed around him, as it had done whenever he listened closely enough, almost from the moment he had discovered its soul, the one that lived and breathed and revelled in its *own* reality. And yet...suddenly...he was desolate. Having come to the end and fulfillment of a rainbow dream he felt drained and empty, as though this one triumph was all he could ever expect from his life.

You don't have to be so cautious with your heart, Nicky, he heard his mother say. *Don't be afraid...*

But he was terrified, not just afraid, and he had no idea why, only that there was in the back of his mind an undercurrent of blind panic that in daylight crept up on him when he wasn't looking, and again in the ebb-tide of the night when sleep would desert him, leave him staring up into the dark.

Don't be afraid, Nicky...don't be afraid...

Windy went walking every day. Hours and hours in the hum of his City, trying to drown the panic, and the feeling that he had been blest to the detriment of those in greater need.

Sometimes, when his friends came calling, he fled into corners of his house where he wouldn't hear their knock on his door or the sound of their voices...guilt-ridden and exhausted...

It never occurred to him that he was the one they always came to in need, that *they* would have moved heaven and earth to give him Peace, if they had known. It didn't work that way in Windy's head.

He sat on a bench on the harbourfront, well away from the shops and restaurants and pubs that catered to the gentry, the elite gone looking for some dangerous and strange and one-of-a-kind to satisfy the end of *their* dreams. Nicholas Wyndham found himself without any dreams at all, yet with no sense of loss, nor a fist-clenched rage at having been wronged in any way...and still the emptiness clung to him...gnawed away at his soul. Something had come into his life, or perhaps gone out of it, and he had no idea what it could be.

The tides moved against the sea-walls and embankments; the sun stretched lengthwise across them, golden in the morning light and blood-red in the deepening shadows of evening. If anyone in passing took notice of a young man dressed for a different time and place, their regard made no dent in the depth of his despair. He had moved, all unknowing, beyond their everyday, into a wasteland he never encountered before.

Diana went looking for him...used a key each one of his family of friends kept tucked away for when he might not be home and they needed a place to hide away from their own homes. The sterile silence scared her, yet she went from room to room, upstairs and downstairs... found him sitting in the garden with a bottle of wine beside him...two others empty at his feet...

"Windy..." she said, but Windy wasn't really there to hear her voice, or be aware of her shoulder when she raised him up from his chair, took him upstairs and put him to bed, wrapped herself around him.

"Whatever it is, Windy, we'll take care of you," she whispered.

He put his face between her breasts and silently prayed she wouldn't let go.

They all huddled in his music room; down the hall he tossed and turned and wept in his sleep. Brandy was beside herself, the inclinations of her own nature making his discomfort so unbearable that she fled from them to be closer to him. Diana said nothing, looked at the place where she had been and of a sudden found it impossible to chasten her for being so much of who and what she was. The rest of them sat quietly, a respectable portion of Windy's wine cellar in attendance upon their complete bafflement.

"...Ever since the performance of his symphony..." observed Thomas somewhat cryptically.

"What, ever since?" demanded Diana, who was by her own admission always too quick to be critical of almost everything.

"You know what I mean," replied Thomas.

"No I don't, Tom," she said. "I understand that *something* changed after the performance, but I have no idea what it was or what you're talking about."

Thomas shrugged. "Well in that case maybe I don't have any idea either," he said.

They glared at each other across the small circle they'd all made, sitting cross-legged and sprawled on the rug beside the clavichord. Brandy appeared in the arch from the hallway.

"He stopped crying," she said, but it was obvious to everyone that a moment of rest for Windy had brought her no peace at all. She wriggled a place between Andrew and Gareth and looked miserable beyond belief, leaned into Andrew's arms and quietly took up where Windy had left off.

"We have to start at the beginning," said Alain hesitantly. "We have t'figure out how and where it began."

His recent arrival on the scene made everything he said rather tentative, yet he managed to provide a much-needed objectivity when their passionate regard for each other tended to obscure clear thinking.

"Well..." said Gareth. "The symphony then. Windy was nervous and excited beforehand, but afterwards..."

"Exactly," nodded Alain. "And so were we...all of us. He'd not given any of us even a hint of what he'd done...and then there we were, watching him, the orchestra following every move and gesture he made—"

"—And every note seemed to go straight to my heart," whispered Brandy from Andrew's shoulder.

"Windy was talking to us," he said, stroking her hair. "And it wasn't just for those of us who know him, either...it was for everyone there..."

"It *was*...for everyone," murmured Diana.

There was a rustle behind one of the large potted *ficus* trees on either side of the windows overlooking the Mews. A rusty brown brush of a tail crowned with chocolate raised itself up out of the corner; a cinnamon-coloured dog-fox preceded it into the proceedings, went sedately to where he could curl up in front of Gareth, then slowly bent amber eyes to each one of them in turn, lifting a glistening nose up in some sort of vulpine greeting. At the archway into the hall, Zoraya appeared as if by magic.

"Windy is different from all of you," she said, before she strode past them and went downstairs. "He's sleeping quietly now."

Hasan shifted up onto four paws and padded after her, noiselessly.

"How does she do that?" Diana asked Gareth.

"Why is Windy different?" asked Alain

"Does anyone else think that fox is spooky?" asked Thomas.

Eventually, they decided that around-the-clock attention was called for where Windy was concerned, at least until such time as whatever affliction had come upon him was recognised and in some fashion ameliorated. Thomas volunteered attendance through the night, but only after Brandywine had been promised he'd not leave him for any length of time longer than calls of nature or maybe a quick run to the wine cellar. Diana said she'd be back for breakfast and a morning watch, and kissed Brandy on the stairs as they all trooped away into the night. Left alone, Thomas went down the hallway and arranged himself quietly in a big armchair beside Windy's bed, surprised himself with the rush of warmth he felt looking down at a familiar face grown drawn and haggard with distress.

"If it's something any one of us has done there's no need t'spare our feelings, Nicky," he growled softly, and stopped himself a hair's-breadth from trying to smooth it away. "You've always been here for us when we needed you...and I know you'd die rather than accept our thanks or gratitude for what's in your own nature, but you need t'let us know...if you can...so we can help with whatever it is..."

Alain lay down beside Andrew and drew the blankets up around them, put his head down where Andrew could stroke his hair and hold on to him at the same time.

"I don't know him the way you do," he whispered, "but it's so dreadful to see him hurting so much and all of you hurting for him. What'd Zoraya mean when she said he was different?"

Andy shook his head.

"I don't know I wish I did," he said. "Windy's older than all of us, but not by so much it should make this kind of difference...whatever this kind of difference is...the one that's causing him so much hurt..."

Alain put his arms around Andrew's waist and buried himself against his chest.

"I hate it how it hurts everyone so much. I wish I knew something that could help..."

Andrew put his nose in Alain's hair and was grateful no one could see his face in the candlelight of their bedroom....that Alain was there at all....

"That's how I know you belong with us," he whispered.

Diana climbed the stairs to her loft, knowing full well there would be no sleep for her between that moment and the morning, when she would go back to the Mews to let Thomas go home, and keep watch on Windy until someone else came along to do the same.

She undressed and lay across her bed, the moonlight sneaking through her windows to streak across her body...surprised to find a thought and an image of Nicholas Wyndham in her swimming consciousness.

"He's not for you," she said to no one. "You don't love him or want him that way, but you would die without him, Diana Morrison, for sure you would die without him in your life..."

She lay a while longer in her bed...got up and dressed again...

Thomas likely would have fallen asleep by now. Someone *responsible* needed to be there...

Gareth closed the stable doors quietly behind him, followed the flicker of candlelight and the click-clack of the loom Zoraya had brought to his studio. Hasan lifted his head from up where he perched on a rafter, eyes gleaming down in candlelight reflections as he passed beneath him, stretched himself down to the hand that came up to scratch one ear long enough for the lamps of his eyes to sneak back into the dark as he not-so-spookily went back to Snoozeland. Gareth sighed.

"Zoraya..." he called.

"Here, my prince," she called back to him.

She worked in a pool of light, her hands moving quickly back and forth with the shuttle and her bare feet working upon the treadles of the loom. Before her a cloth of some ancient gossamer and dream became real, patterned with swirls of desert sand and moonlight.

"He's different," said Gareth. It was all he could manage just then, watching the light play upon her skin, knowing that no chocolate had ever been so sweet as the taste of her in his mouth. She nodded, looked at him over her shoulder, for a moment, before going back to her work.

"Yes, my love," she said, "and it is for me to make him comfortable with what has come rushing into his world."

Gareth only watched her, already knowing full well that if it had been some sort of Destiny or Fate or Magick that had brought her to his dreams and thence into his life, it was also for this purpose before all of them—to bring Peace to the one who had looked after them all and let them breathe.

"This is the *Weight of the World*," she said.

Hours later she came to bed and made love to him. Hasan awoke only for a moment, before his eyes closed again and those two beneath him drifted into sleep.

Brandy stared out into the night, in her garret room high above the City. She fought terror and heartbreak and willed herself not to go rushing back to the Mews...

She knew something was in the wind of change upon them...the possibility of something she had dreamt of and never dared hope to ever become real...

She cried herself to sleep, her head bent against the glass of the window that looked down upon the world outside.

The next evening and one they watched Zoraya seemingly float down the hallway to Windy's bedroom, the fox Hasan at her heels, and her shoulders draped with a thing of gossamer and dream, that carried faintly the whisper of wind across the desert, and all that had come before or would ever be again. When she returned her shoulders were bare, and the fox curled himself at her feet as she sat beside one of the windows of the music room.

"He has never known real sadness. What he feels now is the suffering and despair of people whom he has never met, yet whose cries of anguish fill the air around him, deafen him, blind him to all the things that are good in this world, all the good he has done.

"When he made the music we know as his symphony, it was Windy taking all of the sorrows and sadness you have ever known in your lives, to give it back to you as something beautiful and light enough to be borne...to give you Peace and Joy of it...

"In doing this he opened a door to something he himself had never known and it was more than he could bear on his own...more than he could have survived alone, without all of what you feel for him in your hearts to keep him here in this world.

"I have left him with the *Weight of the World*...now it is for all of us to lend ourselves to him, help him lift it away from his soul, so he will become again what he was...for all of us..."

Evening drifted slowly into Night, wore on with only a word or two from any of them to break the Silence, or a rustle of clothing when one of them would be roused to walk down the hall to where Windy lay beneath the coverlet Zoraya had woven for him. When they awoke, the first light of the day had come upon the windows of the music room, and Zoraya was gone with her spooky fox, but someone they knew as Windy stood in the archway, with the *Weight of the World* at his feet.

"She told me not be afraid," was all he said, and he smiled for the first time in weeks.

Fata Morgana

for Fritz and hearts mended

Spring sprang, and seemingly overnight all signs of winter melted away, leaving the City bathed in a spate of sultry weather more midsummery than mid-April. In early morning the sun appeared to leap into the sky, and smile benevolently before bestowing its regal solarity upon the world. On such a morning, reminiscent of one a year past, Windy was roused up from sleep by a different kind of humming in the air, something not of the City, but rather of those who lived and breathed within it.

From the vantage of his music room windows he could look out over St John's Mews, past the fresh new buds of the apple trees around its perimeter, and see an almost unbroken parade of neighbours and strangers out on the Boulevard, all in some odd but recognisable sort of pilgrimage to wherever it was they were going. He dressed slowly, fascinated by the tide of humanity moving past the archway, and, as he slipped one last button on his trousers into place, saw a small group of pilgrims come away from the others, and recognised his friends.

"Windy come quick something's happening!"

It was Brandywine of course, rushing ahead of the others, her face glowing with excitement, and Diana not far behind, racing long-legged after her, shaking her head.

"Brandy, something's always *happening*," she cried, laughing. "You don't even know, so why're you so excited?"

The rest of *les Boulevardiers* followed more sedately, but with no less enthusiasm. Brandy spun around and danced until Diana caught her up, and then, arm in arm they led their contingent to the cobblestones beneath his windows.

"What's going on?" he called down.

"Something in the harbour...again," informed Thomas.

Windy did a rapid head-count.

"Where's Gareth and Zori?" he asked.

Andrew shrugged. "We stopped by the studio but they were gone."

Alain slipped an arm around his waist and added, "They left a note...it said *Come to the harbour*..."

"Did they leave a note for the entire City?" Windy asked incredulously, lifting his gaze back to the unbroken tide of citizenry yet streaming past the entrance to the Mews.

Alain was the youngest of them all save Brandy. He grinned, and it was an enchantment, a mirror of her own delight in the extraordinary. Windy was down his stairs in an instant, but as they came to the entrance to the Mews, Brandy saw a stout, cassocked figure standing before the doors of the church.

"Come with us, Father!" she cried. "There's something happening at the harbour."

Ambrosius shook his head, not so much declining her invitation, but more as though awakening from some personal reverie. Brandy leapt up the stone steps to take his hand.

"Come with us," she insisted. "Please. It will be wonderful, whatever it is..."

The priest allowed himself to be led down the steps, where he was promptly surrounded, regaled and in all wise welcomed as they all rejoined the hejiraic flood, content to be drawn along whether it took them to the harbour or not.

At length they arrived, stood amongst hundreds that lined the sea-walls and embankments, marveling at *what was happening...*or what had happened, and now held them all in disbelief and wonderment.

Out past the enclosing arms of the bay, on the horizon where the ocean swept away to join with the sky, a city shimmered in the morning sun, minarets and towers raised up into the light, all seeming to float above the water's surface on a cloud of silver and diamonds and gold.

"I've never seen anything like it...!"

"It can't be real..."

"Of course not it's a mirage...an illusion..."

They stood and listened, no less awed by the clarity and seeming reality of what stood out to sea before them, but silent with a prescience that the explanations being offered all around them were far too convenient. Thomas, being the tallest of them, scanned the crowd, found at the forefront of the onlookers a familiar head of gingery hair and beside it a crown of dark glistening curls.

"I think I can see Gareth and Zoraya," he said, and immediately began a polite but inexorable progress towards them, drawing everyone else along in his wake. They turned as he boomed out a welcome from twenty paces, Zoraya's smile showing a brilliant white in the dusky serenity of her face, Gareth seeming to be almost dozy in sleep-dreaming.

"Now we can go," he said, when they were arrived beside them.

"Go where?" asked Brandy.

Zoraya called for Hasan, who appeared an instant later from out of the crowd behind them, and leapt into her arms, his cinnamon-and-chocolate brush coiling round the waist of her white *kandura*.

"How does he do that?" asked Diana.

Zoraya's smile grew wider. "Hasan can be wherever he pleases to be whenever it pleases him to be there...and seen only when he wishes to be seen."

"I think it's magic," offered Alain.

"Perhaps," said Zoraya. "Nevertheless, it is Hasan...and now you must all hold to each other's hands..."

Gareth led them in this exercise, and once they all were joined in such wise to one another, closed his eyes. The others followed suit. Hasan might have chuckled in a foxy sort of way, and Zoraya laughed, whispered something that sounded very much like *abracadabra*...

...So that when they opened their eyes, they no longer stood amid the throngs of the harbourfront, rather in a courtyard much like the Mews, but flagged with great slabs of polished stone—marble and porphyry—veined with ribbons of gold that glinted and shone beneath their feet, and surrounded by palm trees whose fronds high above them moved in a gentle breeze spiced with the breath of the ocean now at their backs.

"Are we where I think we are?" asked Thomas.

Having been there where the *where* was once before, though now it was there rather than somewhere else, Gareth seemed to stop being so dozy and nodded.

"We are," he said, "and so is everyone else from the harbour, except they're *not quite* where we are."

Zoraya said, "You are not being so helpful, my love." Hasan leapt from her arms and raced across the courtyard to where a large grey cat could be seen returning from the water's edge with a goodly-sized fish of some sort still wriggling in his mouth.

"It's Grim!" cried Brandy.

"Hasan has been told he must not chase the cats," said Zoraya reassuringly, "and we all are here, as we are everywhere all at once, even in those times when we are not aware of being anywhere at all."

Diana said, "So a minute ago we...being those of us here now...were together on the sea-wall...but now we're not...or we still are, but we're here too?"

She looked thoroughly confused. Zoraya smiled. Hasan went nose to nose with Grim for a moment; then they turned and trotted side by side to join them.

"Are we going somewhere else now?" asked Andrew.

"*You* are not going anywhere without *me*," said Alain with great conviction.

"That is perfectly reasonable," said Zoraya. "Let go your hands from all but yourselves."

She closed her eyes in their direction, and both Andrew and Alain slowly seemed to grow ghostlike until they faded away entirely.

Brandy went wide-eyed with surprise and fright, letting go of Diana's hand. Both of them misted away together. Gareth and Tom and Ambrosius got translucent in their turn, and dissolved in the light. Zoraya turned to Windy.

"You know it is not needful for you to go?" she asked.

Windy nodded cautiously, said, "Maybe I'll just stay here with Grim and Hasan?" and sat himself on one of the stone benches that rimmed the courtyard. Fox and cat did dreadful things to the fish.

"Where have they gone to?" he asked.

Zoraya smiled sleepily.

"Wherever their hearts have decided to take them."

Windy got drowsy. When he woke up, Zoraya was nowhere to be found. The scintillant haze surrounding him was comforting, but also quite warm. While watching Hasan and Grim in their somewhat unnatural camaraderie was, to be sure, quite diverting, yet he felt a bit at sea with everyone else gone off to wherever they'd gone. Just about that time, it occurred to him that he was quite thirsty, and noticed cat and dog-fox, having made grisly work of the fish Grim had extracted from the ocean, now ran about with muzzles all a-drip with droplets of water.

He rose to follow them about, and found them returning to a shallow, but apparently spring-fed pool hidden away in a corner of the courtyard, enclosed by a low ring of polished marble. He sat beside the pool, leaned forward to splash some water on his face, and was surprised to find he had no face at all...or at the least...nothing in the way of a face he could find reflected in the pool. Puzzled, he leaned closer, found himself gazing down into an endless starburst of pulsating light that was very familiar... enticing... mesmerising...and then he slipped headfirst into the pool.

At first, finding himself almost waist deep in snow shrieking down out of the skies in a decidedly blizzard-like fashion, Thomas was inclined to be more than a little bit huffy... until he realised he wasn't at all cold, or even mildly dampened by the snow that seemed intent upon burying him and the world around him. Thereafter he became philosophical.

"Given that I was just standing in the middle of a mirage, this really isn't anything to get worked up about," he said out loud. Then too, the overwhelming nature of the storm itself reminded him quite vividly of a night not so long past, that had been a preface to and an agent for his introduction to a crotchety old bookseller.

He looked around in search of something else besides snow and vaguely discerned a darker something-or-other no more than a few hundred yards away, from whence came what he thought might very well be an alluring voice he had heard before, now calling to him again. He became, for the second time that day, an inexorable thing of forward motion, and at length came to large outcropping of rock as yet un-buried by the snowy deluge. A darker shadow revealed a cleft in the monolith, and as he inched himself sidewise into its shelter, the storm without became a whisper, and the shadows slowly (and with no apparent cause) divested themselves of darkness enough that he could see a doorway at the end of a long stone-walled passage. Being polite upon occasion, he knocked before entering, and found himself in a small but cosy room, candle-lit, with a fire blazing on a hearth at the far side. A woman sat in a rocking chair beside the fire, looked up at him and smiled.

"There you are," she said.

"So it would seem," replied Thomas noncommittally.

"Can I help you?"

She was perhaps forty-five years of age, greying dark hair framing a small elfin face that was also quite familiar to him.

"I think I'm looking for someone," he said.

The woman smiled again. "I'm afraid she's not here just now," she said apologetically, "though I *am* expecting her."

"Maybe I can wait?" he said, looking around for somewhere he could do just that with a small modicum of comfort. Unfortunately there were no other furnishings in the room.

"Probably not worth your time," said the woman gently, "especially when it's really just a matter of *you* deciding when the time is right. And then again, there seems to be a question of just who it is you're really looking for."

Thomas said, "I wasn't aware of that."

"Well...these little glimmers of revelation do tend to move along at their own pace."

Thomas nodded. "I imagine they do—"

"There!" she cried. "You've just had a glimmer!"

"I have?"

"Yes indeed! You've imagined. *That* is a wonderful beginning."

"If you say so."

"You don't have to take my word. You'll find out for yourself soon enough."

Thomas couldn't remember how he ended up back out in the snowstorm.

Alain whispered, "Andy, are you all right?"

Andrew said. "I think so. Where are we?"

Alain shrugged and grinned.

"Together."

"That's good....but where are we together?"

"Somewhere."

"That's pretty vague," said Andrew. "It doesn't really clarify much...."

Alain refused to be intimidated by inference or ignorance, but remained steadfastly cheery. They sat alone, side by side in a small room with two walls lined by decidedly uncomfortable wooden chairs. A third wall held a doorway, that both assumed was how they had come into the room in the first place. The fourth wall held yet another doorway flanked by an official-looking counter, behind which sat an official-looking person of the female persuasion.

"We're almost ready for you," she said brightly. "Just a few more minutes. Have you all your paperwork in order?"

"Of course," said Alain.

"We do?" asked Andrew.

Alain leaned sideways and kissed him. "Yep. Got everything we need right here," he said, and patted his jacket pocket.

Andrew was mildly astonished.

"I didn't even know we were gonna need paperwork."

Alain's grin returned.

"That's why we're good *together*."

"Do we know what the paperwork is for?"

"Of course," said Alain, again.

"Right," said Andrew, "but are we sure we wanna do this?"

"It's not for a while yet, Andy, but we both fell in love...and they said as long as we checked out okay then there was no reason why they couldn't come to live with us..."

Andrew mulled that over. "It's settled then," he said, reassured.

"Not quite yet," said Alain. "But someday."

Andrew nodded. "Brandy will be proud of us."

The official-looking woman called their names. Hand in hand they stood up, allowed themselves to be ushered through the door beside the official-looking counter. In the room beyond was a long table behind which two men and three women beamed at them as they entered, but they had eyes only for the three-year old twins sitting hopefully in front of the table.

Andrew said, "Good morning Stella. Hiya Jamie."

Alain didn't say anything, knelt down and grinned his usual when Jamie and Stella rushed into his arms.

Nicholas did a slow somersault into the blaze of light, landed softly on his back staring up through all the light he had blazed through a moment before. It was very comfortable.

He contemplated simply staying where he was in spite of the obvious precariosity of not knowing quite where it was he was...but decided there was an inference to be made—that nothing occurred without a reason, and he had yet to discover the reason or reasons for any of the most recent nothings that had come his way.

He got to his feet and began to wander. The interesting thing about the light blazing around him was that it blazed at a short distance from him wherever he was at any given moment; that he was moving around in a bubble within the light, which allowed him to make observations regarding what might appear before or around him.

He also noticed that the air/light hummed; that it was what he imagined might be the sound of an engine or some such contrivance that produced blazes of light...and bubbles within them...and that prepared as he might have been for portents and wonders, open-mindedly as was his nature, still he found himself somewhat awed.

This feeling became more intense when through the blaze...the effulgency...he saw a figure approaching him whom he recognised almost immediately.

"I found her," said Robertson.

He stood to one side and Windy saw him take the hand of a young woman whose name had been Rochelle de Montenay.

Ambrosius was terrified. He had only just gotten used to the idea that somehow, he and *les Boulevardiers* had been transported into the middle of an impossibility; now he felt himself to be free-falling through a void, through coruscations of light and darkness, but nowhere to be found a place of stable up-or-down.

After a while, one can only fall so fast, yet he felt an acceleration of his descent with every passing moment, until he was falling so fast that the nothingness around him became motionless to his dazed senses. Thereafter he floated, and at length came to a slowly revolving whirlpool of emptiness that laid him gently down between a pair of comfortable-looking armchairs, one of which was already occupied.

"There you are," said an echoing sort of voice. "Can I offer you a glass of wine?"

Ambrosius trembled. The face from whence came the offer of refreshment looked down upon him, ancient, bearded, hawk-like and thoroughly forbidding...yet, looking up, he saw the features soften, and a mischievous smile come through the wealth of whiskers.

He struggled to his feet, tottered there for a moment before a nod of the other's head offered the vacant chair. Gratefully, he accepted, but took great care not to look at anything except his host, because he knew for a fact they were surrounded by a void of immense proportion, and felt that paying any attention to it might just precipitate him back into free-fall.

"Where are we?" he asked hesitantly.

"Wherever you'd like us to be," came the thoroughly unenlightening reply.

"Am I dead?"

"Not yet."

Ambrosius let out a cautious sigh of relief, reached into a fold of his cassock and brought forth a handkerchief to mop the perspiration of Fear from his forehead.

"I'm sorry," he said at length. "I've spent more than a year trying to come to terms...but I failed a young man miserably...and in the process I'm sure I offended you...that I've fallen from your Grace..."

The bearded, hawk-like and thoroughly forbidding face softened...the dark eyes became bottomless as the priest sought some kind of comfort from them.

"I think we have made a tyranny of your Word," he said brokenly.

"*My* word?" said the ancient. "I suspect I am not who you think I am, Ambrosius."

"Then who are you?"

The face smiled. "Surely *you* would know that better than I, since I can only be what you envision me to be."

Ambrosius felt the unseen world unravelling around him.

"Do you mean—?"

The face nodded.

"Yes. Exactly. Would you like that glass of wine now?"

Brandy felt a moment of panic from being nowhere, and then she was somewhere—a hillside meadow bathed in sunlight, carpeted in lush green grass and spring flowers... daisies and bluebells and black-eyed Susies—overlooking a vale wherein was nestled a small cottage in the crook of a meandering stream.

From below came the sounds of the crowded garth-yard fenced round the cottage—a handful of sheep, goats, a pair of milch-cows...she thought *I know this place*...though she could not say how or why...

But as she descended the hillside, all colour and sound seemed to flee away from before her, become sepia-toned and silent, like one of the new "moving pictures" that had become the rage. Magically, the garth-gate opened before her, and she thought...again...*I know this place*...

Nor did she have to enter the cottage to know that she had come back to her first home; that inside, her father sat beside her mother in their bed, who had fallen dreadfully ill, but had struggled to survive that their baby might come into the world.

She heard their silent tears...watched as her father took her up from her mother's arms...and she did not need to follow him to a doorstep in the City, or as he staggered back to the desolation of his loss, and realised, almost gratefully, that he too had fallen victim to the illness that had taken her mother.

Brandywine realised she had been dearly loved; that she had not been abandoned at all.

Diana took a minute or two to still the sudden pounding of her heart. Moments before she had been holding hands with Brandywine and Andrew, but now they were nowhere to be seen and she was standing in the middle of a shaded alleyway she assumed to be somewhere in the City she had never been before.

The walls to either side of her showed nothing but timeworn brick; the cobblestones beneath her feet were worn down enough that what once had been rounded surfaces now melded smoothly with the comfortable level of moss and what-not between them.

It was strangely quiet. Strange because the cobblestones spoke of a great deal of traffic over the years, yet the alleyway appeared to have had no visitors in quite some time.

That was when she noticed it wasn't really an alleyway. For it to have qualified as one, it should have had at least one way to leave. Hers did not. The pounding of her heart resumed in earnest, accompanied by an old memory that rose up suddenly...of an alley she had known quite well in a forgotten dream. She turned and breathed a sigh of relief to see a familiar door in the wall at its other end...walked slowly towards it...turned the handle...stepped inside... found herself in a small but cosy room, candle-lit, with a fire blazing on a hearth on the far side. A woman sat in a rocker beside the fire, looked up at her and smiled.

"There you are," she said.

She was perhaps forty-five years of age, greying dark hair framing a small elfin face that lit up at the sight of her.

"Hello, Mum," said Diana.

Mum smiled even more.

"Hello, my love," she said, rising to embrace her.

Diana felt her knees going weak, the pounding in her heart become painful with wishing and hoping and the nagging thought in her mind that she was smack in the middle of something that should have been another dream if not for its thoroughly disconcerting *realness.*

"I miss you so much," she said. "I have so many things to tell you..."

Her mother shook her head. "No you don't, sweetheart. Do you think I've not been listening to you at night before you fall asleep? Do you think I don't know all the things in your heart...?"

"Mum..."

"Hush...come sit with me next to the fire..."

Diana knelt beside her and fell into the warmth of the arms around her, that was so much deeper than any fire could bring to her soul.

"I love you, Mum," she whispered.

"There was a young man looking for you not long ago," said her mother.

Diana closed her eyes...

Gareth said, "They're all going to be totally disarrayed by all of this."

"Not at all, my prince," said Zoraya. "Your friends are entirely more resilient and accepting of the inexplicable than you give them credit for. In the end we all shall be together again, and the mysteries explored will have made endless horizons for us to seek out in the realms of Real."

"You're amazing," said Gareth.

"Only by your courage and vision," she said. "This freedom you have given back to me is something must be shared. It is how Life continues on regardless of what may rise up to challenge it."

"It's been a while. Maybe we should go back?"

Zoraya smiled. "Do not worry, my love, it has been but a breath of Time..."

...That ended with them blinking in sunlight, surrounded by hundreds of others who stared out to sea, where a city of towers and minarets slowly faded away into the morning mist. Slowly these folk went about their business, one by one or in small groups, no one of them unchanged by the mystery of their shared experience, even if they might not come to realise it for the days and weeks and months to come.

Thomas said, "Well...that was interesting...though I have no idea why I'm so tired."

"Must be from slogging through all that snow," said Diana knowingly. She slipped one arm through his. "Perhaps a bit of bed-rest is on order?"

Thomas looked only mildly surprised, and they went off together. Andrew and Alain seemed preoccupied.

"Don't we have somewhere we have to be just now?" asked Andrew.

Alain said, "Not where you think."

"But someday, right?" said Andrew.

Alain nodded. "Someday...but for meanwhile..."

He grinned, elbowed Andrew gently and they walked off together along the Promenade, turning to wave goodbye, promising surprises in the near future. Ambrosius followed them with his gaze until they were out of sight, remarking cryptically...

"I have a great deal of *re*-thinking to do."

...Before he scurried off, sandaled feet barely touching the paving stones in his haste to re-think thoughts that had been provided for him and his brethren for a millennium or two. Hasan winked into foxiness at Zoraya's feet, as a great grey tom-cat leapt up onto the Promenade with a fish still wriggling in his mouth. He sideways bumped the dog-fox conspiratorially before they too wandered off.

Gareth said, "I think it's time for breakfast," and Zoraya only smiled sleepily and allowed herself to be led away in search of the cheese-gooey biscuits she had discovered to be her favourite morning food...which left Nicholas and Brandy alone on the embankment.

"Did you have an interesting time of it?" he asked.

"I did," she nodded happily, "but I still can't figure out why you decided to jump in the water, Windy. You're dripping wet, y'know. Somebody needs t'take you home and change you into some dry clothes."

Nicholas looked down at himself, all sea-sodden and bedraggled, and couldn't help but agree with her.

"I can't imagine who *that* should be," he said cautiously.

Brandy walked herself into his arms, laughed as they headed homeward to the Mews.

"Oh Windy, now I'm all soggy too," she said with absolutely no dismay in her voice, "but you *squush* when you walk...you do...really...listen..."

The Unfading Flower

for Teelie

At 11.47 on a bright sunny morning towards the end of May, a group of seven young men and women charged down the pavement of the Boulevard. After waving a greeting to the white-cassocked cleric who smiled benevolently down upon them from the door of the Church of St John the Defender, they turned onto the cobblestones of St John's Mews.

Leading them was a tall woman with a close-cropped cap of dark hair, her brown eyes flashing with excitement as long, smooth-muscled legs encased in silver dancer's tights carried her forward over the cobbles, and the stylishly ragged hem of her white linen shift

swirled about her thighs. Following her were four young men in fawn-coloured morning coats and trousers, three with small leather portfolios tucked under their arms; behind them was a dusky-skinned young woman of mystical appearance, in flowing white robes, attended by a large dog-fox loping at her side and the last of the faun-coated young men. Following all of them was another young woman in a brilliant yellow sun-dress whose deep green eyes looked anxiously towards their destination as the sun glanced blindingly off the thick honey-gold curls of her much longer-than-shoulder-length hair.

Together, they negotiated the narrow lane of the Mews, until they came to the wide circular court at its end, where apple trees rose up against the surrounding walls and filled the morning air with the sweet scent of their first blossoms.

"Has anyone actually spoken with him in the last week?" asked one of the formally- attired young men. His dark almost black eyes were filled with concern and his pale almost delicate features—starkly contrasted by the jet black colour of his hair—wore a worried frown.

"Surely you've seen him, Brandy," said the girl in the dancer's tights, addressing her companion in the yellow sun-dress.

"I haven't either, Diana," she said with a touch of what was half annoyance and half worrisomeness. "I've been busy painting ever since I got my invitation, I didn't want to disturb Windy, and I've not seen anyone at all. Tom, what about you?"

"Not me," replied a second morning coat, shaking his head of longish brown hair. "Been cleaning up that story I'm going to read, and watching someone practise a dance routine. How about you, Gareth?"

Gareth waggled his head of flame-red hair and began to polish his spectacles in mid-stride.

"I thought Andrew was looking after him," he said, referring to the concerned fellow who had begun the conversation. "But can we please get on with collecting him? I've got to have my case of sculptures and Zori's weaving delivered to the palace grounds *before* we go off for that bit of lunch..."

He took Diana firmly in hand and led them across the courtyard, to where a pair of leaded windows stood open above the dark oak door facing the court, and the soft strains of a harpsichord trilled out over the hum of traffic on the Boulevard.

"Windy! Are you up there?" cried Brandywine, calling up towards the open windows.

"Of course he's up there," Diana said impatiently. "Silly, who d'you think is playing the harpsichord?"

"Di, quit being a bitch to Brandy and go on in," said Gareth. "We'll be here all day if we wait for him to come to the door."

"By all means, do let us go inside...at once if not sooner," grinned Thomas Beverley. "While all of you are dragging our virtuoso from the harpsichord, *I* shall ferret us a bottle of his Rhenish from the wine cellar."

Andrew MacKinnon frowned again and expressed doubts as to the wisdom of such a course. Alain seemed agreeable, but Gareth seconded him at once.

"We haven't time, you sodden beggar," he said, pushing Diana towards the door. "Drink all you bloody want at lunch, but let's get him out of here and be on our way..."

A few moments later all of them stood at the top of the stairs leading up to Nicholas Wyndham's bed- and music rooms, finding him hunched over the keyboard of an ivory-inlaid harpsichord that dated back almost three hundred years to the reign of James the Fourth. Wyndham looked up from the sheet of staffed paper beneath his right hand and smiled faintly.

"Hi," he said, as his left hand fell away from the keyboard. "I didn't think I was going t'see any of you today."

The seven at the head of the stairs exchanged puzzled glances. Brandy took a hesitant step forward.

"Windy you've got to hurry," she said. "Gareth's got t'get his sculptures to the palace and Zori's got her weaving...and then we're going to have lunch before the audience starts."

Nicholas smiled again, running a hand through his pale blond hair as he shook his head.

"I've decided not to go," he said softly. "Besides, this piece I'm working on is almost finished and I really don't think I should just run off and leave it..."

Nicholas stared past Diana and Brandy to where the others were trying to fit his cello into a case belonging to the viol; then he looked down at the keys of his harpsichord, played an aimless trill of notes with his left hand, and sighed before looking up again, at Diana's determined face and Brandy's sun-browned expression of near misery.

"The reason I'm not going to the audience," he said slowly, "is because I've not been invited."

"Nonsense!" exclaimed Diana.

"Windy no...!" breathed Brandy.

To his vast relief, Tom, Gareth and Andrew left off trying to fold his cello and stared across the room in disbelief. Zoraya seemed unconcerned. Windy nodded to all of them.

"It's true," he said apologetically. "I didn't get an invitation."

"Well you're coming with us anyway," Diana decreed, straightening up and indicating that the desecration of the cello should continue. "Yours most likely was lost in the mails, is all."

A murmured chorus of assent went through the studio, but Nicholas remained seated at the harpsichord, shaking his head.

'Invitations and letters from the Amaranth Palace don't get lost in the mail, Diana," he said. "And even if mine *did* get lost, I'd not be allowed through the gates without it.'

"But we could explain, Windy,' said Brandywine desperately. 'We could tell them what must've happened and they could find your name on the list and—"

Again Nicholas shook his head.

"It wouldn't work, Brandy," he said softly. "I could be anyone, no matter who you and the others said I was. The Guard couldn't risk that..."

Brandy looked round at the others helplessly.

"Then what're we gonna do?" she said. "We can't just troop off and leave you here all by yourself."

An uncomfortable silence filled the room as they looked at one another but not at Nicholas. Finally, he did for it with a snort of laughter.

"That is exactly what you *are* going to do," he said with a grin, "and you needn't be looking like the world is going to come to an end because of it. Do you honestly think I'll be hurt if you go without me...or that I'd want you to miss the chance of a lifetime—to perform before the Queen!—simply because blind Fate managed to make off with my invitation? Gods! but it's a deadly poor friend I'd be to all of you if I expected *that*...!"

He stood up from the harpsichord and rescued his cello under the pretext of herding them all back down the stairs.

"Windy we couldn't—" declared Andrew.

"All for one and one for all," intoned Thomas. "We'll just get pissed as newts and forget the whole thing."

"The devil you will!" swore Nicholas. "You all look perfectly splendid and you're going t'knock the knickers off Queen Caroline whether she wears any or not, so quit pretending this means nothing and be certain you'll be telling me all about it tomorrow."

Diana paused at the top of the stairs and Brandywine clung to his arm.

"Windy are you sure...?" they asked in unison.

He hugged them both, kissed each on the forehead and smiled.

"Positively certain," he said. "Now go on, all of you, and do your very best...for me..."

He stood at the stairhead for a few moments after they had gone, briefly heard their dismayed conversation as they retraced their steps back to the Boulevard. Then he went back to his harpsichord, began working on the second movement of his concerto in D major...found he no longer had the heart to continue.

Thank the gods I convinced them to go without me, he said to himself as he went to his windows and looked down on the apples trees ringing the courtyard. *Maybe there'll be another gala sometime soon...*

For the better part of an hour he stared sightlessly out into the courtyard, trying to swallow disappointment...and hoping each of his friends would do well that afternoon. He didn't hear his front door open again, or the soft footfalls on the stairs. When finally he turned away from the windows, Brandywine was standing beside the harpsichord with tears in her eyes.

"I couldn't go without you, Windy," she said. "I just couldn't..."

He said her name, once, hoarsely, barely heard above the pounding of his heart.

"It's not fair," she said softly, shaking her head. "You're better than all of us, Windy. You're the one made us all sing..."

He said, "Please go it's not too late, Brandy, please..."

She shook her head again, took a rectangle of heavy lavender paper from the pocket of her sun-dress and slowly tore it in half, leaving both pieces on the polished walnut surface of his harpsichord. Nicholas leapt forward, horrified, as she turned away from him, looked down at the riven invitation with its royal proclamations scripted by hand in purple ink:

The presence of
Miss Brandywine Lloyd
is hereby requested
to display the products of her Art
before
Her Sovereign Majesty
Caroline de Montigny
at two o'clock
on the 7th day of May
on the reception grounds
of the Amaranth Palace

"Brandy you didn't have to do this..."

"Yes I did!" she cried, turning back to him with a fierce light in her eyes. "The Queen would never have taken any notice of my silly drawings and paintings anyway...but you...you, Windy...your music... I would have been so proud of you, and it would have been horrible to be there without you, knowing you were here...alone...pretending not to be disappointed so everyone else could go..."

She seemed lost in the middle of his music room, suddenly a small child for all that she was grown, with tears streaming down her brown face and the yellow sun-dress now the saddest sunshine imaginable. Nicholas felt a wrenching in his heart, like an invitation on lavender paper torn in half.

"I can't help it, Windy," she sobbed, her fingers twisting at the cloth of her dress. "We're all such children...but you look after us. You make us believe we're important, help us to believe in ourselves, and you never stop, Windy...you never stop loving us even when we're being stupid or cruel or selfish you just make sure we can all go home at night knowing we're not alone.

"I've tried t'be just like you, Windy, but I can't! I love Zori and Gareth, an' Andy and Alain...so very much...and Tom and Diana, even when she's being dreadful...but not like I love you..."

She stood in a wash of sunlight, brighter than the light that shone down on her, like one of her paintings an intimation of something infinitely less complicated than lives lived listening to the drumbeat of what passed for civilisation.

"Windy, don't you understand?" she cried. "It would've meant nothing to me if you weren't there t'be the best of us all."

Suddenly he did understand, or felt he was closer to understanding than he'd ever been before. He nodded his head looked down at his feet.

"Branny I'm an idiot," he said softly, "and too much of a coward to stop pretending to more than I am, or using all of you as an excuse.

"You're the one who's better than all of us, because the only thing that matters to you is caring about everyone but yourself. Oh we all smile indulgently, and tell ourselves your kind of caring is sweet and charming, that we're all above that sort of thing...so very sophisticated...while the real truth is that there's not one of us worthy to even crawl at your heels!"

She shook her head wildly, desperately.

"Don't say that, Windy, please don't, because it's not true at all. I'm so selfish. I love you more than any of the others. I don't want anybody else to have you, and—"

She stopped, pressed her hands to her lips, terrified by what she had said, her eyes staring at him as though he'd slapped her; and he, stunned by something so obvious, reeled drunkenly as her words echoed over and over in his head. He looked up at her, and she had not moved. They stood prisoned in their own squares of sunlight, she like the sunshine itself, but with fear and sorrow creeping into her eyes with every moment he stood silently. He tried to speak, but found that the welling of relief inside him would not allow it; that its very intensity frightened him into silence. He clenched his teeth, forced the words to come from his lips.

"I love you too, Brandy," he whispered. "I've always loved you..."

He felt his knees folding under him at the immensity of the thought, the feeling of mad exultation mixed with something wistful, almost sad, now that they had passed from Innocence to Knowledge. He sat on the hard polished floor with his head bowed, and the music room was a dry empty desert around him until she knelt beside him, put her arms around him.

"What do we do now?" she whispered.

"I was hoping you would know," he said quietly, "because nothing and no one will ever change you from who and what you are; but all of a sudden I have to be somebody else. It's not a bad thing, but everything is so different now..."

He clung to her as dust-motes and springtide danced in the air down around them, and he felt wealthy beyond any of his dreams, wreathed in the apple-blossom scent of her skin and her hair.

"Then we'll just go on doing what we've always done," she said, "and that way neither one of us will be lost..."

The Silver Rose Café was almost deserted, the white linen cloths on the tables fluttering forlornly in the soft breeze, the serving staff standing around aimlessly, knowing full well where all their usual patrons had gone, but mildly stunned by such wholesale desertion.

Nicholas and Brandy sat alone on the terrace, wishing they might eat and drink more, if only to banish the almost comic discomfiture of the staff, yet still somewhat light-headed with the wonder of their discovery. At whiles, a motor car would go by on the Boulevard, but to the two of them the world seemed to exist at some immeasurable distance, far and far away from where they sat together at their small table.

"It's like the whole city has gone to the palace," she said, sipping at her glass of wine. She glanced shyly at him over the rim of her glass, and a small worried frown creased her forehead. "Windy have we done something terrible? Are we going to lose them all...?"

Nicholas tossed a handful of bread crumbs to some pigeons on the sidewalk, stared into his own glass.

"I don't know," he said; and then, fervently, "I hope not. I guess we could go on without them, but it wouldn't be the same...like it was some dreadful price we'd had to pay so we could be...y'know..?

She nodded.

"Maybe they already know?" she said hopefully.

"Maybe," he said. "Lately I've been getting the feeling I've been kind of blind to a lot of stuff that wasn't really all that difficult to see. Maybe we're not giving them enough credit, though; maybe we're the only ones who haven't known..."

Guilt and empathy for their waitress kicked in and they ordered the rarely-if-ever-available-on-the-menu *Fruits du Roi*—a soup plate of lemon ice buried in blueberries, cherries, strawberries and tiny orange slices, all crowned with fresh whipped cream and chilled Armagnac drizzled down over top of everything. Then they spent the next half hour waiting to see who would be the first to drip the cream down their front...which Brandy did when the attention she was paying to her spoon was drawn by someone else seated on the terrace.

"Windy look!" she breathed, staring wide-eyed over his shoulder as a dollop of cream disappeared between her breasts. "Oh damn I can't go fishing for that out here Windy isn't she gorgeous...?"

Without being discourteously obvious, guised in concern for the errant plop of whipped cream, he managed to turn in his chair and cast a sidewise glance at the young woman who had been the cause of the disastrous disappearing dollop; found he could do nothing but agree with Brandywine. As she excused herself to go off in search of the powder room—or somewhere she could go without embarrassing herself whilst removing the chilly bits down her front—Nicholas continued to stare at the newcomer to the café, wondering who she might be and how she had escaped his notice in the past. The logical answer to the latter half of his question came to him immediately—that the woman had not frequented the Silver Rose, nor could not have done so without being remarked upon by himself or his friends or someone of their acquaintance.

"And that would be an impossibility," he murmured aloud, "because even a blind man could not fail to be dazzled..."

The irrationality of that thought was lost upon him as he studied her—lustrous brown hair falling about her shoulders that shimmered with glints of burnished copper in the sunlight, framing a delicate oval face with finely-chiselled features, and lips that were full and curved in a slightly amused smile. Her dress was impeccably tailored in some rich plum-coloured fabric, and on her left breast she wore a large purple blossom whose fragrance, even at a distance, was intoxicating.

And then, perhaps sensing his interest, she raised up a pair of luminous violet eyes, and acknowledged his attention with a slight nod of her head. Nicholas smiled apologetically, turned away as Brandy returned to their table.

"Isn't she marvellous?" she asked softly. "I can't tell you where I've been after that whipped cream, but...Windy...have you been rude? She's staring at us!"

He owned to having committed a slight indiscretion.

"I don't mind if you look at other girls, you know," she assured him, "though I think I'd be horribly jealous from now on if they stared at you."

Nicholas frowned. "Then I'm going to be jealous of almost everyone in the City because they all stare at you."

Brandywine blushed.

"Don't be silly," she said. "I'm not half so pretty as anyone—"

"Then they must stare at you because they know where you went to find that whipped cream," he laughed, "and wished they'd been there to help."

They had hours of daylight left. Brandy sipped the last of her wine and dared spoon the last of the *Fruits du Roi* in such a way she could share it with him.

"What shall we do? Where shall we go?"

"Let's go everywhere," she said. "Like the night we followed you all over the City. Everything will be brand new again..."

"Everything and everywhere then," he said, rising from his chair. He paid their bill on their way off the terrace, carefully polite and trying not to look back at the woman still sitting alone there.

I hope the others are doing well," Brandy said as they reached the sidewalk. "Windy, could we walk by the palace...just to see...?"

He turned to her with concern.

"Are you sorry you didn't go with them?"

She seemed startled by the question, a look that disappeared in a radiant smile.

"Not at all ever," she said, hugging him.

They went off with their arms around each other's waists, and two lustrous violet eyes followed their progress down the Boulevard.

The reception ground of the Amaranth Palace was a riot of noise and colour. The broad green lawns that swept back from the wrought-iron fences encircling it were filled with bright-painted pavilions topped by gaily-streaming pennons, and an uncountable number of cream-and-lavender-coated retainers, and artists, musicians and writers come from the farthest corners of the kingdom in answer to their sovereign's invitation.

Nicholas managed to find them a place in the vast milling crowd at the fences, and there Brandy stood in silent wonder, pressed against the iron bars, her eyes shining with excitement, drinking in the sight and sound of it all, and the splendour of the palace itself where it rose up behind the celebrants.

"Oh Windy it's incredible!" she breathed. "And look see, there, at the foot of the steps! That must be the Queen, sitting beneath the purple canopy with the gold border!"

For as long as he had known her, Brandy's near child-like appreciation of the world around her had been a source of delight to Nicholas, something that had marked her at once in his eyes as someone rare and special, for all that the quality seemed absent in himself. At whiles, when her outstretched hand or cry of amazement would distract him, he looked away from her, but it was not for any great length of time and he realised, for the first time, that his enjoyment was more to be found in watching hers—in the breathless parting of her lips, the sound of her laughter, the sweetness of her innocent pleasure.

At length, they came away from the palace grounds, and bought honey crisps in paper cups from a vendour beside the canal, before wandering off to the Emerald Gardens where they spent an hour watching children with their kites, and Brandy fell in love with a flop-eared spaniel puppy who decided to tag along at their heels until his person—a pixie-faced little boy in grass-stained trousers—came to collect him.

From there they went to the Zoological Gardens, where she shivered when the tigers roared at them, but refused to leave until they had roared again...three times...and then had laughed at a brown bear cajoling papers of honeycomb from its audience.

When a small child in a sweet-stained frock happened to pass by, tearfully berating the equally small miscreant who had stolen her ice cream cone, Brandy promptly extracted a trice of coins from the pocket of her sun-dress and sent her off to buy another...with chocolate and cherries on top...

And the day slipped slowly away behind them, until the sun dipped down over the river, turned into molten gold whispering through the City, and the air began to grow chill with the coming of evening. As they sat on a wooden bench on the Promenade overlooking the harbour, Nicholas gave Brandy his coat and put his arms around her, losing himself in her warmth and her nearness as the river close by sang its way past them to the freedom of the ocean.

"You're the most wondrous girl in the world," he said.

"So long as you think so I'll be the happiest," she said.

"We've not gone anywhere near everywhere and everything."

"We can try again tomorrow?" she asked hopefully. "And every day after that? We've got lots of time, Windy..."

She snugged herself closer to him and sighed.

"Let's sit a little while longer, and then we can go home? I'll make tea and bake biscuits and maybe you can make the City sing again..."

It was dark by the time they neared the Church of St John the Defender, where it stood guard over the entrance to the Mews. The Boulevard and the City seemed utterly still, as if having partaken of the sense of peace that filled them both. As they reached the stone arch over the cobblestones leading to the courtyard within, Nicholas stopped suddenly, and Brandy looked up at him, puzzled.

"What's wrong, Windy?"

"I'm not sure," he said quietly, looking back over his shoulder. "Do you remember the woman we saw at the Silver Rose?"

"How I could I forget her...!"

"I could be wrong, but I think she's been following us all afternoon...and just now I thought I caught the scent of that flower she was wearing on her dress."

"But why would she be following us?"

He shook his head in reply, and peered back along the shadow-lined sidewalk of the Boulevard, until he saw a cloaked figure standing a block away, just beyond the circle of light cast by a streetlamp. Even as he watched, the figure began to move towards them, until at last they could plainly see it was indeed the woman of the café, now with a dark-coloured mantle about her shoulders. She seemed to float along over the pavement, her progress almost ghostlike as she went from light into shadow and back again. When she was no more than a handful of paces away from them she stopped, and smiled apologetically.

"Forgive me," she said. "I've been following you, and now I am discovered at last...but please, it was no more than an innocent fancy. You see, I am in many ways new to the City, and the two of you seemed so charming, so much at home. I thought to follow in your footsteps and so encounter only those sights truly worth seeing."

Her smile grew more relaxed when neither Brandy nor Nicholas evinced any displeasure at her confession. She offered her hand to each of them, introducing herself.

"My name is Marie Santinelli," she said, bowing slightly. "Am I forgiven my presumptuous behaviour?"

"I think we're the ones should beg forgiveness," said Brandy, "for staring at you so shamelessly this afternoon. I'm Brandywine Lloyd—it's pronounced more like Brandwin without anything in the middle—and I didn't mean to be so rude."

"And I'm Nicholas Wyndham, who could not help being so. May we atone for *our* sins by asking you to join us for tea?"

She sought to hide her smile at his compliment, and then, after briefly considering, accepted the invitation with a small inclination of her head.

"You are very kind," she said. "I should be pleased to join you, but only if you are sure I'll not be an inconvenience."

Nicholas bowed grandly from the waist.

"Not at all, m'lady," he said. "If you would but come with us, we are no more than the hop of a frenzied kangaroo from my door...but please keep a watchful eye lest we are taken unawares by the great and terrible Grim the Grey."

Brandy giggled, shoving him forward as she hastened to explain to Marie Santinelli that Grim the Grey was no more than a large tomcat who lived in St John's Mews and was said to be the "king" of all the cats in the City...and that there were no frenzied kangaroos lived anywhere close by.

"Thank you for enlightening me," she replied with amusement. "I had been crushed were I to have passed him by without a proper acknowledgment of Sir Grim's exalted station. Lead on if you will, Master Wyndham, your lady and I shall follow at our leisure..."

"...Miss Santinelli, I do hope you'll excuse Windy. He's not usually so silly and—"

"You must call me Marie, now we are friends," she said, "and I see no reason to excuse him for anything. I have said you both are quite charming, and I say it again."

They sat in the front parlour while Nicholas attended to the tea, comfortably settled on the divan while a small fire crackled in the grate. Brandy blushed at their guest's words and hastily changed the subject of their conversation.

"If only we had known you could have joined us for the whole afternoon," she said. Marie shook her head kindly.

"No, my dear, that would have been impertinent of me. The two of you seemed happy enough in each other's company and I would not have intruded."

"Oh we wouldn't have minded at all, Marie. Windy and I have known each other almost forev...well...two or three years, anyway..."

"But today was a special day, was it not?"

Brandy could only nod, and Marie smiled with an air of satisfaction.

"I knew it at once," she said. "One would have had only to look at you to see that something greater than friendship bound you together today. You both are every bit as beautiful as your City."

"Do you like it?" cried Brandy. "It's such a wonderful place to live, and it never seems to change from being wonderful. Oh everyone and everything gets older, of course, but whatever it is that makes the City what it is stays the same. If you're happy it's happy right along with you, and when you're sad it somehow manages to make the sadness less hurtful.

"I know I'm not explaining it very well. I guess what I really mean is that it's a *kind* city, like it *cares* about the people who live in it..."

Marie nodded.

"How strange you should say that, Brandywine," she mused softly. "I felt the very same thing on the day I arrived here."

"And it's a very magical place, too."

"Really...?"

"Yes it is. Amazing magical. Last summer the City actually *sang*...at least that's what it sounded like. And Windy was the one who discovered the song, though he'll never admit to it."

"I remember reading something of it in the newspapers," said Marie. "And you say your Nicholas was the mad musician then?

Brandy nodded proudly.

"Then why was he not at the Queen's audience this afternoon? Surely he, of all the musicians in the kingdom, should have been there."

Brandy cast an anxious glance at the door to the kitchen, where Nicholas was just then readying the "tea things" on a tray.

"He never got an invitation," she whispered. "We all of us got ours—I mean me and Diana and Tom, Gareth and Zori, Alain and Andrew...our friends—but Windy's didn't arrive, and I tore up mine because it didn't seem fair..."

Marie looked at her incredulously.

"Well...I didn't think the Queen would miss my silly drawings, and Windy was so disappointed that he'd been left out..."

"I think your Windy is a very lucky young man," observed Marie quietly.

It was then that Brandy decided Nicholas was taking far too much time bringing their tea, excusing herself hurriedly, but with one last word before he went off to help.

"I'll see if I can persuade him to play for you," she said. "Then you'll know why I wouldn't go without him."

Eventually, Brandy lit candles and tea was served upstairs in the music room, while Nicholas tuned a great Hibernian harp and began to play for his attentive audience of two. With Brandy and their guest enthroned upon a mound of pillows on the floor, his fingers drew deep thunderous chords from the instrument, and gentle trills that seemed to fill the room like the heart-songs of an ancient land, until the room no longer could contain so much joy or sorrow and the music spilled outward through the open windows and down into the courtyard below.

All three became lost in the sound—there has never been a single instrument that evokes long-forgotten memories so well as the harp of Hibernia—and the rich fragrance of the purple flower upon Marie's breast twined itself in among the notes and set them to dreaming lotus-dreams of older times and faraway places. Marie rose from her nest of pillows, seemed to float sylph-like to the windows, and there found dozens of listeners perched in the branches of the apple trees and along the top of the wall enclosing the court.

"The cats," she whispered, enthralled by the music and the sight of three-score eyes staring unwaveringly upward.

"They always come to listen when Windy plays," said Brandy, who had risen to join her at the casement.

"Were I one of them I could do no less," said Marie. "There is more magic here, in this place, than in half the kingdom..."

And even when Brandy left the windows, she would not move from them until Nicholas had put aside his harp and, two by two, the eyes winked out as the cats went off to a night of forage and adventure.

"Thank you," she said at last, returning to her place beside Brandywine. "I have never heard the harp played as you have played it for me. Your music is a gift that cannot be returned in kind."

Nicholas merely nodded, wordlessly, like one caught in the toils of his own web of magic, and Marie turned to the girl beside her, questioning with her eyes the tablet of paper Brandy hastily put aside.

"What have you there, Brandywine?" she asked. "Will you show it to me...please...?"

"It's nothing, Marie...truly..." stammered the girl. "I just felt like drawing...with the music...and you... standing at the window."

"Please may I see it?" Marie asked again.

Brandy handed over her sketch-pad hesitantly, holding her breath as Marie, with eyes glowing like twin flames in the shadowed beauty of her face, studied the tracery of pencilled lines wherein she had been captured in the magic of a few moments before.

"May I keep it?" she asked quietly. "So I will never forget the wonder of this night...of you and Nicholas... and the cats. You cannot know what it would mean to me, to have found you both, always to have a remembrance of myself as I've been tonight... "

"But it's only a ragged little sketch, Marie—"

"Yet you have ensnared me in your ragged little sketch as Windy did with his music...captured my soul like a sorceress. Please let me have it...and then I must go..."

Brandy nodded slowly, and carefully put her signature at the bottom of the portrait, along with the inscription:

"Marie in Magic"...with love...Brandy

THE UNFADNG FLOWER

From the door of Nicholas' house they watched her walk away into the night, a dark slender figure disappearing into the deeper shadows of the cobbled laneway that led to the Boulevard.

"I hope we'll see her again, when she's all settled in. D'you think she had a good time? She seemed so lonely..."

Windy put his arm around her shoulders.

"She's got you for a friend now," he said. "And the loneliness will go away the minute you start showing her all the wondrous things you see in the world."

"It's not right she should be that way."

"Not for much longer, Brandy," he said. "You'll see her again soon, I'm sure of it."

They stood awhiles in the doorway, silently staring up at the stars and drinking in the scent of night air spiced with apple blossoms. She turned in his arms and put her head against his chest.

"Come home with me, Windy. Everyone will be here in the morning to look for you...for us...but I don't want to share you with anyone for a little while longer than that, and it will take them longer to find us at my house."

In a small garret room on the edge of the New City, they moved together in timeless dancing that was only for the two them, to music never heard by anyone but themselves, in time to their hearts beating as one, their bodies joined together.

And the earth did not move beneath them, nor could it have done so, for at such times all things are perfectly still save for those who are the dancers.

"...Windy wake up...please Windy wake up fast...!"

He opened his eyes to find her kneeling beside him on her bed, sunlight streaming through the windows of the garret to burnish her brown skin, turn the tangle of her honey hair to a halo of spun gold. He reached for her sleepily, yet remembering the strains of the music they had made together, but the note of panic in her voice made him pause, brought him fully awake.

"Branny what's wrong?"

"Windy I don't know," she cried. "I was sitting here watching you sleep and someone came up the stairs and pushed this under my door..."

He rubbed the last vestiges of sleep from his eyes and from her trembling hand took a rectangle of stiff lavender paper, that bore the following in purple ink:

The presence of
Miss Brandywine Lloyd
is hereby commanded
by Her Sovereign Majesty
CAROLINE de MONTIGNY
in the Royal Audience Hall
of the
Amaranth Palace

"Windy, what am I going to do? Why does she want to see *me*? D'you think she knows I didn't go yesterday? Maybe I was the only one!"

"I don't know what to think, Brandy," he said, trying to still the flutter of her hands," but you must go, of course, there's no doubt of that. You mustn't worry, though. I'll go with you. I'm sure it will be all right..."

"Brandywine," said the Queen, with a smile curving her lips.

"Marie...?" said Brandy.

"..I was curious, my dear," said the Queen, who had been Marie Santinelli. "During the first intermission, my Master of the Guard informed me that all but one of my invitations had been received at the gate. I wished to know who it was who would *not* respond to what most would consider a once-in-a-lifetime honour...and why...and so I left one of the ladies of the court in my place, veiled as I had been through the first performances, and went in search of answers to my questions. The guardsmen I sent to locate you informed me that you—and Nicholas—were at the Café of the Silver Rose, and that is where I found you. I felt so badly when that whipped cream went down your front..."

Brandy blushed furiously, wishing she could disappear into a corner of the small chamber to which they had retired. She who had been Marie laughed softly.

"Your Majesty—"

"You may call me Marie, Brandywine," said the Queen.

"I don't understand...Marie..." she stammered.

The Queen sighed, looked down at the purple flower pinned to the breast of her robe.

"I will answer any and all of your questions, my child. Please don't be nervous. We are friends..."

"Well...Your...Marie...I don't understand how you can be Queen Caroline. She was crowned over sixty years ago. Everyone in school knows that...and...and...."

"I should be much older than I seem to be?" asked the Queen softly.

"Well..yes...I suppose that's it..."

Her Majesty sighed a second time.

"I *am* the Queen Caroline who ascended to the throne sixty-seven years ago, Brandywine," she said. "At the age of twenty, a year older than yourself, forty-eight years before you were born. Contrary to what I may seem, I am eighty-seven years old."

Brandy shook her head in disbelief.

"But how can that be, Your Majesty?" You look—"

"Like a young woman of twenty years," nodded the Queen. "I know. And therein lies a great secret, one I will tell you if you will promise...swear to me...it shall never be told to another soul while I yet live."

Brandy swallowed and nodded her head.

"I won't tell," she said. "I promise."

An expression of pain flitted across the face of the Queen for an instant.

"Always it has been *Your Majesty* this and *Your Majesty* that," she said bitterly, though it was to herself rather than to the young woman before her. "Even among my friends...but you are forgiven, Brandy Lloyd. It's not your fault, I know...however...the secret..."

She turned away and stared at a portrait that hung upon the wall at her back—of her father, King Michael the Sixth.

"For as long as the de Montignys have ruled over this kingdom, there has been in our family's possession a treasure of such priceless worth that no one who was not of the royal blood has ever been entrusted with the knowledge of its existence...until today.

"This treasure—discovered by the founder of our line so many hundreds of years ago, the first King Michael—was and remains to this day simply this flower I wear upon my breast. The ageless Amaranth of legend that shares its name with my throne and this palace. It is this flower, my dear Brandywine, that grants to the one who wears it the boon of everlasting youth. I wear it at all times; when I sleep it rests on my pillow, beside my head...and in all the years I have been the Queen of this land, I have not aged a day beyond the day when my father first placed it upon my breast..."

"Marie," cried Brandy, "why are you telling *me* the secret...?"

The Queen turned slowly to face her again.

"Because I'm tired, Brandy...so tired. Because last night, when you said the City never seemed to change even though everyone and everything in it grew older, you were speaking of my blessing and my curse. Outwardly I've not changed at all, but inwardly I'm old and very very tired...

"You see, I never really had a choice. Just as my father never had a choice when the flower passed to him from my grandfather. He was ninety-seven years old when he gave it up to me! Ninety-seven years, Brandy! And seventy-four of them were spent upon the Amaranth Throne.

"He begged me then to take the flower, told me it had become too much for him to bear; that it was my duty, as a de Montigny, to take it and rule the kingdom for as long and as well as I could before passing it on to my firstborn. I've done that, my dear, but I don't wish it to go on any longer."

"But your child then?"

"There is no child, you know that," she said hoarsely. "Inwardly, even on the day of my coronation, I knew this day would come...but I swore the one who followed me would have the choice I never had; that someone other than a de Montigny would sit upon the Amaranth Throne for no other reason than that he or she loved this city and this kingdom enough to do so by choice.

"My true purpose in inviting the artists, musicians and writers of this realm to *entertain* me was to find such a person, because the day-to-day details of running a kingdom must also be done with an appreciation and respect for the souls of the people who live there...for the things that cast light and promise and goodness on each and every aspect of their lives. Words. Music. Ragged little drawings by people who have nothing but Love in their hearts.

"Brandy, I want you to sit on the Amaranth Throne. I want you to be the one to look after our country..."

The silence became tangible, crowding round Brandy as the Queen's words thundered in her head. Then she laughed...wildly...

THE UNFADNG FLOWER

"I can't be a queen!" she cried. "I...I don't know anything I'm not even a real artist...or anything at all...I wouldn't know where...or how—"

"Brandywine, look at me," commanded the Queen. "There are ministers and counsellors who know how to look after the details, to do the things that are necessary to keep this land healthy and at peace with our neighbours...but there is only one thing a king or queen *must* know...one thing only...and that is how to *love* those who are in their charge, to take the advisements of her counsellors and then decide what is best for her *people*.

"When I left the gala yesterday afternoon, I wanted to know why my invitation had been spurned; why you had not answered a summons most others would have died to receive...and I found you sitting at a table in a café with someone who should have received an invitation but somehow had been overlooked...someone you loved enough to give up a chance at being recognised as the wonderful and talented artist you are. I watched you, and I realised your love was really the only thing that mattered to you, that it extended to spaniel puppies, great roaring tigers, dancing bears and a small child who had lost her sweets...and even to a complete stranger who lied to you about being a newcomer to the City...

"Love is all you will ever need to guide you, Brandy. If you do nothing but love, as you've always done—deeply and from the very bottom of your heart, without a cruel thought even for those who have used you cruelly—then you will cast a light from the throne that will brighten the lives of all my people. Will you...can you do this?"

She looked up at the Queen with tears in her eyes—that always came so easily and seemed to be no more than a foolish girl's weakness, but were in fact the measure of her greatest strength—and could find no answer to the question.

"I would have to live here then," she murmured. "Here in the palace. And I would have to guard the secret because I promised. No one could know..."

"But you would be the Queen, Brandy, and the promise then could be made by another of your own choosing, someone worthy of keeping it for you as I know you will keep it for me. That much I would allow you surely...so Nicholas and your friends could be near you..."

Brandy's eyes began to shine through her tears.

"Windy could be the Royal Musician," she whispered dreamily. "And Diana and Tom and Gareth and Zori and Andrew and Alain...they could be Royal everythings too. Would that be all right...?"

"Of course it would be all right," said Queen Caroline, reaching to take the young girl in her arms. "Who would dispute such things, that could do nothing but add brightness to the world...?"

And Brandy smiled to think of it, each of those dearest to her accorded the honour and recognition she knew they deserved so richly. And then she frowned, and a look of utter desolation clouded the brightness of her dreaming green eyes. She moved away from the embrace of her friend with an image of Windy in her mind, as she last seen him, before the doors to the audience Hall had closed behind her...and she shook her head.

"Your Majesty...Marie..." she said softly. "Please come to visit me every day. I'll never tell anyone who you are, I promise...but I can't be the queen for you. I know it's so terribly selfish but I can't.

"Please may I go home now?"

Her Sovereign Majesty Caroline de Montigny nodded her head once, in silence, and Brandy walked to the door of the chamber.

"Brandywine...?"

"Yes, Your Majesty...?"

"You almost said yes. Will you tell me what changed your mind?"

Brandy nodded hesitantly.

"I couldn't...I couldn't stand the thought of watching Windy grow old while I stayed young...and then losing him," she said, and she went out through the door, closing it softly behind her.

For a very long time after the girl had gone, Her Majesty the Queen sat in her chair and moved not at all save where her hands twined restlessly about a tattered silk handkerchief she had drawn from a fold in her robe. Her eyes stared sightlessly into space, dreaming of a face and a voice from her own past that had faded into silence almost a lifetime ago... remembering now only the words of the golden-haired girl who had gone:

"I couldn't stand the thought of watching Windy grow old while I stayed young..."

"Even as I could not bear the same thought of one who might have given me another child," said Caroline de Montigny in a whisper.

And a single tear welled from one luminous violet eye, to fall upon the unfading flower upon her breast.

Envoi – The Shape of Things to Come

"...Windy, are you sure it's okay?"

They stood at the music room windows overlooking the Mews, the apple trees filled with cat-faces keeking out into the early morning light, and the gaily-decorated tables awaiting only the arrival of guests to become the scene of celebration. Brandy turned to him, let fall the bedsheet she'd worn from the bedroom, put her arms around his waist and her head against his chest. He got lost, in the scent of her, the warmth of her body against him.

"It would only be for tonight."

He nodded into her hair, knowing he had come to a place in his life where he could never deny her...anything...and that the inclinations of her generosity and goodness could only serve him as a signpost to his own sense of safety and serenity.

"She said she would come?"

Brandy nodded, didn't look up. "She said it would be the very best way she could imagine to spend her last day..."

"And you're sure it's what you want to do?"

She nodded again, this time raising up her emerald eyes, that shone with the gentle green passion of her infinite kindness.

"You'll help me?"

"Of course I will...all of us...you know that..."

"I do," she said softly. "Windy can we go back to bed for just a little while? I never told you, but after I ran away from the orphanage, I used t'come here all the time...and then, for a while, before they came to fix it all up for you t'find, me and Andy lived in a corner of the stable in the back garden. We always felt so safe here... and now all of us are safe here..."

"All of us," he said. "And you know...I never told you...but before I came to the City, a fortune-telling woman told me that spirits would come to sleep in my bed and bring me Peace. I didn't realise she was speaking of brandy and wine..."

She lifted up her head and then clung to him, pressed against his chest, and he had to change his shirt after she'd stopped crying.

Just before noon a carriage clattered into the Mews, and she raced to find him so they could welcome the couple come a day's journey and then some to be there. Brandy became shy, hung back as Windy embraced his parents.

"Thank you so much for coming," he said to them.

"Oh Nicky...is that Brandywine?" breathed his mother. "She's adorable..."

"She is," Nicholas nodded. "She's...I don't know...I don't have any words that are any good to describe her..." He shrugged. "She's Brandy...our heart and soul..."

He turned to his father, still somewhat daunted with a child's awe of someone who had been larger than life for most of his life...awkward for a moment before he walked into his arms.

"So where's the rest of us," he asked.

"Your brothers?" his father snorted. "Back where they belong, looking after pennies so your mother and I can comfortably be about the business of living, and so they'll have some extra coins in the cashbox to make them feel like they've accomplished something.

"She's quite the little beauty, your girl... Introduce us, find me something to wash some of the dust from my throat, and then give us a tour."

Windy grinned. His mother swept past them, took Brandy in her arms and said, "Now you belong to us. My name is Alexandra...you can call me Mum if you like."

There was still an hour or so before any of the other guests were expected to arrive, so his parents were escorted to a guest room (with a quick dash to provide refreshment) and then given the tour.

"I'm sorry it's taken us so long to visit you," said his father, once he and Nicholas were settled at an outdoor table awaiting the rest of the invited celebrants. "Truly sorry to have missed your concert, but your mother said there'll be many more, so I'm not feeling too badly.... Meanwhile..."

He shrugged towards the perimeter of the Mews, where Brandy and Alexandra were trying to coax a kitten from one of the apple trees. Windy put his head down and smiled.

"She wanted me to remind her to tell you that she'd seen Camille Ardrey at the market last week; that what you'd written about in your letter to her was perfectly fine and to go ahead with whatever you felt was appropriate."

Windy nodded and observed it was a welcome message. His father looked curious.

"Nothing momentous," said Nicholas. "Cami's brother Alain lived just on the other side of the courtyard, but when he passed not long ago he made me the executor of his estate without really saying he'd had family in the Carillon. That's why I was up in the spring, to try and find out if he'd left anyone behind more entitled to look after his property. My letter to her was to ask if her brother's house could be turned into a shelter for whoever was in need of a place to stay. That sort of thing, y'know..."

Frederick Wyndham inhaled some cognac fumes and sipped from the rim of his glass.

"And you'll be looking after that?"

Windy shook his head.

"Not me...but you'll meet the man who asked if it could happen, and he'll be the one looking after the day-to-day."

His father settled back in his chair, looking up past the towers that stood just outside the borders of the Mews...unbroken blue sky...

"You've done so much here," he said softly. "And you're happy."

It was the statement of a question in need of no answer at all.

"Your mother wanted to be sure. She said we'd waited long enough to let you find your feet...that this would be a perfect time to visit."

"It *is* perfect, Da," said Windy, attending a bit to his own glass. "All my friends have found their feet as well...and I've got Branny...and there's a lot of stuff in the wind, but in the end it's all been good. You and Mum have made it so easy for me. I don't know how to say thank you enough."

"Nicky you're my son. I've got three other sons who I love, but what they want out of their lives is pretty simple, in line with what most people feel is a just reward for time served. You've always been different....and I know it was your mother gave you the curiosity and the spirit to have brought you to where you are now. But don't ever ever think you were a burden because of it. I'm proud of you. You've always been *all* the things I've ever wanted in a son...and now I'm thinking you and that lovely girl of yours are going to be the ones who show me a real future for the Wyndhams. The two of you are the ones going t'make it all worthwhile. Just don't say anything to your brothers..."

He grinned and inhaled more cognac.

"...I was painting on the Promenade," said Brandy. "Nicholas bought three sketches and then he came back the next day. He's the sweetest kindest gentlest anything I've ever known...along with my Andy. He's the one getting hand-fasted today..."

Mrs Frederick Wyndham cuddled the little tabby they'd "rescued" from the apple tree.

"He's got three older brothers, you know," she said, teasing.

"I'm sure they're all just as wonderful, but I don't want anyone but him."

Alexandra laughed softly. "His father will tell you his brothers are a pack of philistines, and mostly it's true. They're all very competitive and intent on making the Wyndham legacy bigger and better than how it found them. But when

Nicky came along, suddenly Frederick saw something beyond what had been before, started thinking that perhaps your *Windy* was the one to carry on the real *spirit* of what had made his family in the past.

Brandy blushed. "We all of us call him Windy, I hope you don't mind."

Alexandra Wyndham smiled. "I'm so pleased you're the one who decided to take care of my little boy. And I may have to bring this little wean back to the Carillon with me. I know a magnificent great creature named Amadeus who would love to carry her about."

Brandy scritched the small thing between its ears. They listened to it rumble with pleasure.

Brandy said, "But we have to make sure it's okay with Grim..."

Alexandra cocked her head to one side, making a question. Brandy blushed again.

"I know it sounds silly, but here in the City, Grim is the king of the cats. He looks after all of them, so we *have t'make sure* it's okay..."

Alexandra Wyndham found herself faced with a small miracle of something beyond her ken. She touched Brandy's face, traced a fingertip across her lips, all the while her eyes never once moving from the green gaze of her youngest son's beloved.

She said, "My sweet girl..."

Thomas and Diana arrived. Gareth and Zoraya. Friends of friends. And passersby... strangers...who heard music (a string quartet from the symphony) and laughter come out from the Mews and wandered into the courtyard out of no more than idle curiosity. All were welcomed. Brandy came up beside Nicholas and said:

"Windy, where's Andy and Alain? We can't start without *them*...and who is that funny little man over there...in the brown coat...just come into the courtyard...?"

Nicholas put an arm around her shoulders.

"His name is Teodor Alexeyev," he said. "Not too long ago we knew him better as Father Ambrosius."

Brandy was incredulous.

"He looks so different...so happy now...as if he'd never been—"

"—Father Ambrosius at all," finished Windy.

Brandy nodded.

"I think it's precisely *because* he's not Father Ambrosius anymore that he seems so happy; that now he's free to be true to his own natural goodness, rather than having to justify and preach submission to 'God' as way of dealing with *our* failings."

"What happened?"

Nicholas shrugged. "I think that thing last year with Andy had a lot t'do with it...and this summer, when you carried him off to the harbour with us...but he said that suddenly he had more faith in himself and the people he knew than he'd ever had in the God he came to know in the seminary. And he's going to look after Robertson's place, as a shelter for anyone in need of a place to sleep or a meal or just someone to talk to."

She looked thoughtful, clung to him more tightly.

"That sounds so wonderful...and a little bit sad...is he all right?"

"Better than ever," said Windy. "Wait and see."

"...Is that Father Ambrosius?" asked Diana.

Thomas followed her discreetly-pointed forefinger to the gnome-like man in the brown frock coat and matched the amazement in her voice with his own.

"I'm pretty certain it would be, if he was bustling about in that sackcloth and ashes routine. I wonder what's gotten into him."

"Maybe he's seen *the Light*?" suggested Diana a trifle uncharitably.

"It would be an improvement," said Thomas. "He's not really a bad sort...just a bit misguided."

Diana had to carefully swallow a mouthful of Reisling.

"What?!?!?" demanded Thomas.

"Nothing," she sighed. "Sometimes you're just so...so...*utterly* you."

"And what's wrong with that?"

Diana put her glass down.

"Absolutely nothing," she said again. "Just be quiet and kiss me..."

"...The music is lovely," said Zoraya. "It reminds me of the banquets in my father's palace."

"I didn't know you lived in a palace," said Gareth with an ingenuous wink. "Are you the daughter of an ancient royal family?"

She smiled.

"You are not my prince for no reason."

"I'm not sure I know what that means, Zori," said he.

"That is just as it should be," she replied, and took a morsel of something from her plate that it might disappear in the mouth of the fox at her feet. "Soon there will be many beautiful babies."

Gareth said, "Really? Does that mean something good for me?"

Zoraya smiled her most enigmatic smile and proffered another morsel to him.

"Oh but of course, my love. Making babies can be very time- consuming work...and very *very* serious...or not..."

"Well...I suppose I'll just have to re-arrange myself to take the toilsome parts in stride then?"

She reached out a long-fingered hand and, with one that sparked with a swirling cloud of moonstone set in silver, stroked his lips.

"You are so princely," she said with gentle mockery. "It is almost a pity I have no kingdom to offer you..."

Marie Santinelli was the last of the guests to arrive, only a few minutes after everyone else had sit down to table and the prospect of devouring the immense amount of food and drink that had materialised when no one was looking. She came quietly past the Church of St John, the hem of her purple gown brushing the cobblestones, stopped for moment at the entrance to the courtyard, searching the faces of those in attendance until she found the one she was looking for.

Brandy went to greet her immediately, and burst into tears as they embraced, sniffling their way back to a place at table beside herself on one side and Andy on the other. Windy came to kiss her hand.

"I've brought this for you," said Marie when he had taken his own seat beside Brandy. She handed her a small richly-carved wooden box. "Once I'm gone the palace will be turned upside down trying to find it; for a time it needs to be hidden away and kept safe..."

Brandywine nodded, looking scared.

"You mustn't be frightened," said Marie softly. "All the arrangements have been made. There will be two of my ladies-in-waiting who are more than trustworthy, and they will see that you are introduced to everyone you will need to know."

Brandywine nodded, and continued to look scared. Marie brushed her cheek.

"You are certain you would do this for me?"

Brandywine nodded a third time.

"Windy said everyone will help."

"And tonight?"

Brandy nodded again.

"I must be sure to thank him," said Marie. "But now we are to celebrate...something?"

Later in the afternoon, when all in attendance had eaten their fill and emptied a good many bottles of anything that came to hand, there was a huffing and rustling from he who had been Father Ambrosius. Having done his part to participate in the

216

festivities, he stood a trifle unsteadily, but steadfastly enough to make the following pronouncement:

"It is with an immense and unfailing gratitude for the kindness and generosity of spirit in the young people gathered here today that I am privileged to announce to you all the intention of Alain Devreaux and Andrew MacKinnon to join their lives in the sanctity of their love for each other."

He turned and raised his glass to where the aforementioned now stood in the doorway of Windy's house, both in loose-fitting shirts and trousers of white linen, their heads crowned with wreaths of laurel and asphodel, garlands of field flowers about their necks.

Andrew seemed quite nervous as they approached under the watchful eyes of the more than two-score friends and strangers; Alain only grinned his most dazzling of grins and leaned to whisper words of encouragement to him. Teodor Alexeyev, who had been Father Ambrosius, took them by the hands and led them into the centre of the open space among the tables, faced them to each other.

"By the grace of your goodness and love, I am honoured," he began, and then stopped... briefly... ducking his head to spend a moment with a handkerchief from the pocket of his coat before starting again...

"Do you, Andrew MacKinnon, promise to love and cherish Alain, in sickness and in health, in joy and in sorrow, through the best of times and through the worst of times, for as long as there is Love between you?"

Andrew swallowed and nodded his head.

"I do," he whispered. "With all my heart."

"And do you, Alain Devreaux, promise the very same to Andrew, for as long as there is Love in your heart for him?"

Alain grew serious, but only for moment.

"I do," he said loudly. "With all my heart forever, and a day longer just to make sure..."

Teodor Alexeyev joined their hands together, quickly bound them in a ribbon of white satin, and turned to face the guests surrounding them.

"Well then...it's settled and that's that," he said, and his grin was that of a man who finally had come out from a place of shadows into the light of a new day.

Hasan yipped at Zoraya's feet, made fox-like sounds that might well have been speech, though only she understood what might have been said. In response, Zoraya lifted her head and sniffed the air.

"You are right," she said quietly. "It *is* here. After lifetimes of lost, it has been here all along."

Gareth looked puzzled.

"It is a secret, my prince," she said apologetically. "One I cannot share with you now, though someday I believe Brandywine will choose to enlighten us all..."

The guests, invited and otherwise, were gone. As twilight shrouded the courtyard and the empty tables, a small army of felines came to forage through what would have been, on a day without them, leftovers enough for a week. Once again,

Windy stood at the windows of his music room, overlooking the flutter of tablecloths and the last glints of light on silverware. His mother came silently to stand beside him, put her arm through his and her head on his shoulder.

"Nicky, it was lovely," she said. "So wonderful to finally meet all your friends...and Andrew's Alain is precious...."

"Nothing seems to bother him," agreed Nicholas, "and Andy's said he spends a lot more time smiling at absolutely nothing since they found each other."

"Mister Alexeyev was quite charming."

"Someday I'll tell you his story, and how he came to be himself."

They stood awhiles together, saying nothing, content as any mother and child to simply be close to each other."

"Nicky I recognised her," said his mother at length. "I think she recognised me as well."

Nicholas looked puzzled.

"The one you named Marie Santinelli," said Alexandra Wyndham. "The Queen... Caroline de Montigny...who bid you goodnight with a kiss and took Brandywine with her."

"It's a secret, Mum," he said. "Someday I can tell you, but not just yet. How did you know?"

She withdrew her arm and faced him round where she could put her head against his chest.

"You know I met your father here...in the City. I met him at a gala on the grounds of the Amaranth Palace, when for a short while I had the honour of being an attendant to my Queen. I'm more than twice now as old as I was then...but she has not changed at all."

"It's another secret," he said, resting his chin gently on her head.

He looked out through his windows on the world, and up to where the sky had caught fire in the sunset.

"And your Brandy is friend to the Queen, and today has gone away with her."

Windy nodded.

"For tonight," he said, smiling where she could not see it.

The royal quarters of the Amaranth Palace were as still as the grave with all the servants sent away, drowsing silently into the purple night.

"I'll find the right one, Marie, somehow...I promise I will," said Brandywine.

She stood behind the queen, combing her hair, their eyes meeting in the mirror of the vanity before them. Marie who was Caroline de Montigny nodded.

"I know you will, my sweet girl," said the Queen.

Brandy began to cry. Though hers had been but a short lifetime haunted by loneliness and heartache, in one day she had found two mothers to take away her sorrowing. Marie turned, took her round the waist and pressed her face to the girl's breast.

"I can feel Time crawling to catch up with me," she whispered. "Soon it will race after me, like a hungry animal. I've cheated Time for too long, Brandywine. Now I have only a few weeks, perhaps a month left..."

Brandywine continued to weep into dark hair suddenly streaked with grey and silver.

"Keep the flower safe and hidden. When you are tired and discouraged, a night with it on your pillow will bring you newfound Hope, and a bit more Life added to your natural days."

Brandy nodded, unable to speak. Marie rose to her feet and stood before her, brushed away her tears and took her in her arms.

"Be cautious, my beautiful girl. I know yours is a trusting heart but you must learn caution. My family has tried to reign responsibly and peacefully, yet there have been times when it has been difficult, and even now there are some who would have things other than what they are. You must watch for them, never allow them too much freedom to undo what has always been a fragile balance."

The girl nodded, let herself be led away to the farthest end of the vast bedchamber where an elegant, massively carved four-poster stood flanked by a pair of tall candles sconced on the walls.

"Thank you, Brandy Lloyd," said the Queen. "Now come to bed, and let me hold you and kiss you goodbye..."